Overcoming Sexual Immorality

By

Mary Lozano

Dedication

This book is first dedicated to the glory of the Lord Jesus Christ, One with the Father and the Holy Spirit, who has made me to KNOW Him, His Word, His Ways, and His good, perfect, and pleasing will.

I wrote this book not because I can but because the Holy Spirit can, through me. The only thing I truly know is that "apart from Him, I can do nothing" John 15:5, because we are not sufficient of ourselves, but our sufficiency is in God 2 Corinthians 3:5.

I pray that everyone who reads this book will come closer to the revelation of Him who saves, delivers, heals, and is able to break every yoke that binds you, justify every accusation, and heal every wound… He is the only one who can restore your soul.

Table of Contents

Introduction

There is a war raging all around us that is silent yet savage, invisible yet intensely real. It is a spiritual war that invades every home, haunts every heart, and spans every generation. It is waged with lies whispered into minds, temptations tailored to our wounds, and desires twisted into chains. It is a battle over the very soul of humankind.

Its victims are countless fractured marriages, fallen pastors, weary souls burdened with secret shame, individuals paralyzed by guilt and fear, silently retreating from the light. Satan disguises himself in charm, ambition, flattery, seduction, and even pleasure. His deception is subtle but strategic. He utilizes the desires God has planted within us, such as desires for love, belonging, and purpose. But uses them to pervert them into traps that destroy, not fulfill, causing spiritual erosion, emotional emptiness, and a growing distance from God. This war does not just target the unbelieving. It preys on the faithful, the strong, the seasoned. Those who once walked in truth but grew complacent or distracted. He doesn't just want to lead us astray but wants to destroy legacies, discredit ministries, and derail destinies. What we face is not merely a moral issue or a psychological struggle; it is a profound challenge to our humanity. It is a spiritual confrontation.

That is why this book was written, not as a theological treatise, but as a battle cry —an urgent call to wake up, arise, and arm ourselves with truth. It is for those who are weary of cycles they cannot break, haunted by past choices they cannot erase, or bound by shame they cannot share. It is for those who feel the weight of their family's spiritual history pulling them backward, for those who want to walk in the freedom Christ promised but feel chained to patterns they can't even explain. It is for anyone who knows the pain of fighting in the dark, wondering if freedom is even possible. The enemy knows how to bait the hook and where to strike. His attacks are personal and precise, aimed at the weakest points of our identity, our history, and our trauma. That is why Ephesians 6:12 does not speak of conflict with people but with powers: "For we do not wrestle against flesh and blood, but against principalities... against spiritual wickedness in high places." If we continue to treat this as a natural problem, we will continue to lose a supernatural and generational war. Sexual sin is one of Satan's most effective weapons. It is not just about behavior; it is about bondage. Its roots are buried in childhood wounds, unmet needs, false identities, and family patterns that have never been broken. It hijacks the beautiful gift of intimacy and turns it into a tool of destruction.

The Bible is clear: iniquity travels through generations (Exodus 34:7), so do blessings for those who break the chain and cling to Christ. Galatians 3:13 reminds us that Christ became a curse to redeem us from the curse of the law. The cycle can end and the inheritance change, only if we recognize the roots and declare a new spiritual lineage—one bought by the blood of Jesus.

The fall of spiritual leaders is one of the most heartbreaking consequences of this battle. When those in authority fall, the damage echoes far beyond their own lives.

Congregations scatter. Faith is shaken. Cynicism spreads. But even in these moments, God offers restoration. Psalm 51 is not a story of disgrace but a roadmap to grace. It shows us that confession, brokenness, and honest repentance are not the end of the story. They are the way home.

This is your invitation to explore the roots of your struggles, to identify the lies you've believed, to close spiritual doors that've been left open, and to walk in the authority that has always been yours in Christ. You will be challenged, but you will be changed. You will be convicted and comforted. You will discover that grace is not just enough to forgive you, but powerful enough to transform you. God is purifying His people, calling His sons and daughters to come out of the shadows and walk in the light. If you feel exhausted from the fight, if you're tired of failing quietly, if you're desperate for something real, then this is your moment. You are not disqualified. The same God who redeemed the broken in Scripture is writing your story now. Know you are not fighting alone; heaven fights with you, so your victory has already been won. Let this be the moment you stop hiding and start healing. Let this be the chapter where shame loses its grip and grace takes over.

One of the most potent and devastating weapons in Satan's arsenal is sexual immorality, which has brought down mighty men and women of God. It is a carefully sharpened arrow, aimed not just at the body, but at the soul, the mind, the identity, and ultimately, the destiny of an individual. Sexual sin is not merely an act of rebellion, but a spiritual assault designed to sever our intimacy with God, distort our perception of love, and entangle us in shame that feels too heavy to escape.

In our modern world, with smartphones, social media, and streaming platforms, images and ideologies that once required intentional pursuit now invade our lives uninvited. Lust is packaged in high definition, promoted in algorithms, and normalized in every genre of entertainment. The result? A generation is drowning in temptation while starving for real intimacy. Sexual sin has destroyed ministries, devastated marriages, and decimated the confidence of countless believers. It erodes trust, shatters self-worth, and poisons the well of spiritual authority.

The enemy knows that if he can corrupt someone's purity, he can confuse their purpose, distort their identity, and neutralize their calling. He wants to dismantle you from the inside out. Many who struggle with sexual sin are not simply wrestling with temptation; they are wrestling with trauma, abandonment, and spiritual wounds inherited from generations past. Pornography addiction, promiscuity, and identity confusion often have roots in unaddressed pain, unmet needs, and ungodly soul ties. These aren't just behavioral issues; they are spiritual strongholds that require more than willpower; they require deliverance.

This is why healing from sexual sin is not simply about stopping the behavior; it's about uncovering the root, renouncing the lies, and allowing the Holy Spirit to rebuild the foundations of your heart. It's about understanding the difference between guilt and conviction. Guilt keeps you hiding. Conviction calls you into healing. Jesus did not come to condemn the sexually broken—He came to restore them. And we must talk about spiritual doors. When a person engages in sexual sin, they often open a spiritual door—an access point through which shame, addiction, confusion, and demonic influence can enter. These doors are sometimes opened unknowingly, especially when rooted in generational sin. Patterns repeat until someone, empowered by the Holy Spirit, decides to confront and break them. The blood of Jesus is enough to cleanse, restore, and rebuild.

The Weight of Generational Curses

Exodus 34:7 tells us that God "visits the iniquity of the fathers on the children and the children's children, to the third and fourth generation." This is not about divine cruelty, but a sobering reminder that sin carries consequences that extend beyond the individual. When families leave spiritual doors open through rebellion, idolatry, or sexual sin, those patterns often repeat. Freedom begins with acknowledgment. You must confront the history in your bloodline, expose the hidden agreements with sin, and declare that your inheritance is no longer bondage but blessing. The curse stops with you when you choose Christ.

The Power of Confession and Community

James 5:16 tells us, "Confess your sins to one another and pray for one another, that you may be healed." Freedom flourishes in the light. The enemy thrives in secrecy. As long as you hide, you remain in bondage. Confession, accountability, and godly counsel are the tools that dismantle strongholds.

This journey is not meant to be walked alone. You need a community, not just people who will pat you on the back, but people who will call you higher, who will challenge you to strive, who will remind you of your identity in Christ when you forget it yourself.

The Promise of Freedom

This book is not about condemnation. It's an invitation to freedom, healing, and restoration. True freedom is not the absence of struggle but the presence of Christ in the midst of it. It is walking in the Spirit daily, choosing light over darkness, truth over lies, and purity over compromise.

You will learn how to:
- Identify spiritual patterns and break generational curses.
- Understand the root causes of sexual temptation and immorality.
- Apply biblical truth to areas of personal struggle.
- Build accountability and guardrails that protect your integrity.
- Restore what has been broken through the grace of Jesus Christ.

We are in a time of exposure. Hidden sins are being brought to light. God is purifying His Church, shaking what can be shaken so that only what is unshakable remains (Hebrews 12:27). This is not a time to play with sin. It is a time to surrender fully, to live with integrity, and to be set apart for His purposes. So let this be your beginning of a purified life. Not a life without temptation, but a life filled with truth, courage, and the Spirit of God.

You were not made to be a casualty in this war. You were made to be more than a conqueror (Romans 8:37).

Let's fight. Let's win. Let's walk in freedom together.

Chapter 1
How Sin Entered the Spirit of Men and the Generational Curses that Sustain It

God is the Creator of every living being in heaven and on earth. He created Adam and Eve and placed them in the Garden of Eden to keep them close, to have a strong relationship with them, to walk with them, and to be a Father not only to them but also to all their descendants. Generations have been blessed with His divine presence, purposeful design, and sovereign plans. God has ordained a purpose for every human life, and with that purpose, He has endowed each of us with spiritual gifts with which to fulfill our callings. Furthermore, He granted mankind the power and authority to subdue and steward the earth.

In the garden, Satan approached Eve in the form of a serpent—an appropriate guise, as serpents dwell among the grasses, blending in with their surroundings. He said to her, *"Has God indeed said, 'You shall not eat of every tree of the garden?'"* The woman responded to the serpent, *"We may eat of the fruit of the trees in the garden, but of the fruit of the tree which is in the midst of the garden, God has said, 'You shall not eat it, nor shall you touch it, lest you die.'"* Then the serpent enticed her, saying, *"You shall not surely die. For God knows that in the day you eat of it, your eyes will be opened, and you will be like God, knowing good and evil."*

Though Satan creates nothing himself, he is a master manipulator. He is a liar and a deceiver, skillful in distorting God's truth and design. His objective is to replace God's intentions with counterfeits—anti-designs—that foster confusion, independence from God, disobedience, and, worst of all, separation from the Creator.

We must not live in denial or ignorance of the existence of the kingdom of darkness. It is real. It is highly organized, supernatural, and powerful. It operates with the intent to influence across generations. However, it is *never*, in any measure, greater than the Kingdom of God. That is the defining and eternal difference.

Isaiah 14:12-14

Lucifer, or Satan, as he is better known: "How you have fallen from heaven, O Lucifer, son of the morning! How you are cut down to the ground, you who weakened the nations! For you have said in your heart: 'I will ascend into heaven, I will exalt my throne above God's stars; I will also sit on the mount of the congregation. On the farthest sides of the north, I will ascend above the clouds' heights, I will be like the Most High."

Lucifer's fall from heaven had monumental consequences for himself as a banished angel, for humankind as a now-sinful creation, and for the earth, which became the new stage for spiritual conflict. Cast out of heaven, Satan needed to establish a new dominion, and he chose the earth. He did not fall alone; he brought with him a third of the angels who rebelled with him. More devastatingly, he brought with him his corruption, planting his evil influence into the spiritual atmosphere of the world.

By rejecting God's authority, Satan orchestrated a rival power structure—a kingdom that defies God's will, nature, and redemptive plans. This rebellion led to an ongoing spiritual war between the forces of good and evil. The Devil's mission has always been to oppose everything God represents, and that mission continues to this very day.

His original ambition was to usurp God's authority so that he could "be like the Most High." This rejection of divine rule and the creation of an antagonistic power system are the roots of enduring spiritual conflict. Satan's very existence is now consumed by one relentless pursuit: *dominion.* Dominion across people, across nations, and generations.

This demonic pursuit manifests in what we call **transgenerational influence**—patterns of sin and dysfunction passed from one generation to the next. These patterns may take the form of rebellion against God, deliberate defiance of His will, or behaviors deeply embedded in family traditions and cultural practices that contradict the truth of Scripture. These include addictions, sexual immorality, abortions, and belief systems rooted in unrepentant sin.

Such cycles are not mere coincidences or habits; they are spiritual strongholds, often described in this book as *"generational curses," "bloodline curses," "territorial spirits,"* or *"generational spirits."* These patterns perpetuate dysfunction, causing individuals and families to normalize behaviors that are, in fact, rebellions against God. In doing so, society begins to call *evil good* and *good evil*—a reversal that only deepens the separation from God's truth.

This separation also highlights the consequences of mankind's God-given free will and the sobering potential for even the most divinely crafted beings to choose rebellion and embrace darkness–selfishness, independence, and sinfulness. Contrary to what the devil claimed, after being expelled from the Garden of Eden, the first man and woman experienced death, not initially of the body, but of the spirit. Overcome by sorrow, shame, pain, and fear, they endured what is known as spiritual death. Years later, they succumbed to physical death. Deprived of the Father's intimate presence—the One who had nurtured them with boundless love, they were left to perceive life only through their body and soul, no longer attuned to the Spirit. Adam and Eve began to comprehend the difference between living for good and dying for evil.

What Satan, disguised as a serpent, told Eve was not the whole truth—it was a half-truth, which is often a dangerous lie cloaked in deception. Rather than "being like God, knowing good and evil," as the serpent promised, their pursuit of power and independence cost them their sacred relationship with God. Instead of elevating them, it cast them into moral and spiritual ruin. They did not ascend into divine wisdom but fell headlong into corruption and loss.

Once established on Earth, the devil set into motion a calculated plan aimed at opposing the Creator by killing, robbing, and destroying all that God had made. This was not a random act of chaos but a systematic "anti-design"—a deliberate contradiction of God's divine order. His first and most significant act is to sever man's relationship with God. He demands worship for himself, and tragically, humanity often yields it through sin, whether knowingly or not. Such is the nature of spiritual law.

Though a fallen angel, the devil remains a spiritual being—a prideful son of perdition—who cannot legally operate on Earth without a human vessel. Spiritual beings are unauthorized to act in the earthly realm without a physical body with a will and mind that is surrendered to them. This is precisely why Jesus had to come in the form of a man. Though He was fully God, He had to be born fully human to fulfill His mission legally within the constraints of the earthly realm.

Lucifer's deepest craving is worship, and he obtains it through sin and disobedience to God. Even now, Satan continues to influence mankind by presenting alluring counterfeits of every good and perfect gift God offers to His creation. The tragic irony is that many fall prey to these deceptions simply because they do not believe Satan exists. That disbelief is one of his most effective strategies. When we partake in evil, we open the door to the spirits of darkness, the devil, and his hierarchy of principalities, powers, and rulers who operate with the express purpose to steal, kill, and destroy.

These dark forces rob us of the Father's blessings, which manifest in peace, justice, abundant life, prosperity, familial harmony, mercy, favor, His divine presence and companionship, the fullness of the Holy Spirit, wisdom, and spiritual gifts, among others. These blessings are part of God's covenant for every soul that chooses to walk in obedience and alignment with Him.

At all costs, the enemy aims to extinguish human hope and strip individuals of their sense of divine purpose. He lures people into actions that are destructive not only to themselves but also to those around them. The devil's most cunning and devastating weapon is convincing mankind that he does not exist at all. Yet he does exist—he has established a well-organized spiritual kingdom here on Earth, and this reality must be acknowledged.

Ephesians 6:12

"For we do not wrestle against flesh and blood, but against principalities, against powers, against the rulers of the darkness of this age, against spiritual hosts of wickedness in the heavenly places."

Scripture teaches us that our real battle is not against fellow human beings—be they spouses, children, siblings, parents, or friends. The devil often manipulates situations to stir up strife and division, making it seem as though people are our true enemies. But our fight is spiritual, against the unseen but deeply influential principalities, powers, and rulers that move through the world, perceivable only through our spiritual discernment.

We are spiritual beings, whether we accept it or not, and the greatest battles we face occur within our fallen nature. The enemy works tirelessly to seduce people of all backgrounds into wrongdoing because every evil act aligns us with his fallen kingdom and distances us from God. No man can serve two masters. He either serves God or he serves the devil. The only alternative is the intentional exercise of one's God-given free will—to reject evil, pursue righteousness, and follow the guidance of the Holy Spirit.

Ephesians 5:11

"Take no part in the unfruitful works of darkness, but instead expose them." ESV

In this verse, we are clearly instructed to avoid all association with the unfruitful works of darkness. Yet in today's world, ancient cults and activities have become so popular that we have become slaves to sin and lost in the chaos. This shift has led many into spiritual bondage, distorting our moral compass and numbing our sensitivity to sin. As far as sexual behavior is concerned, anything seems permissible. We live by the popular mantra, "if it feels good, do it"—a belief system that fuels our descent into immorality. This ideology is at the heart of my second book, Overcoming Sexual Immorality.

Before explaining that subject, it is essential to clarify two foundational truths about our spiritual lives—two areas over which the Lord has not given Satan any dominion, among other things, because he does not intrude in them either.

1. The Mind:

Neither the devil nor his demons can read the human mind. Although it may sometimes appear that they can, this illusion stems from their strategic intelligence and ability to observe, study, and exploit human weaknesses. However, demons cannot exercise control over our minds. Every new believer is indwelt with the Holy Spirit, who empowers us to resist the schemes and enticements of the enemy. The only way the devil gains access is if we, by our own will, yield to his temptations and consent to the very things he lures us with.

2. The Will:

Once a man has committed to the power and leading of the Holy Spirit and has fully committed to serve the Lord, the will of man remains outside the devil's jurisdiction, unless it is willfully surrendered. Each of us possesses willpower—the capacity to choose righteousness over sin is enforced by the Holy Spirit who dwells within a believer. With HIM, we are capable of resisting temptation, rejecting ungodly patterns, and making decisions that align with God's Word. However, this 'will' must be cultivated and exercised, especially when confronting deeply rooted behaviors or desires to sin. This is accomplished through consistent prayer, developing a firm knowledge of the Word of God, living a life of repentance, and maintaining an altar before the Throne of Grace, because 'separated from Him, we can do nothing.' John 15:5.

Romans 13:12

The night is far spent, the day is at hand: let us cast off the works of darkness and put on the armor of light.

Romans 6:16

Know ye not, that to whom ye yield yourselves servants to obey, his servants ye are to whom ye obey; whether of sin unto death, or of obedience unto righteousness?

The first step toward becoming a Christian—a true follower of Christ—is confessing Jesus as Lord and Savior. During the prayer of salvation, the individual acknowledges their sinfulness and consciously surrenders their life to Jesus Christ. This is not a mere recitation of words, but an audible, heartfelt declaration that one believes in the resurrection power of God—that He raised Jesus from the dead. That confession, made in faith, results in salvation and initiates a process of transformation. From that moment on, the Holy Spirit, who is the third person of the Trinity, comes upon the believer, empowering their new life in Christ and guiding them through the process of sanctification.

He equips believers to resist the devil's work and assists those who are oppressed by the desires of the flesh and the devil to be set free – delivered. He will do it only for those desperately wanting to be set free and serve God. The Holy Spirit will not intervene in the life of those who are comfortable with sin and are willing to give way to the oppressive demons.

Romans 10:8-12

But what does it say? "The word is near you, in your mouth and in your heart" (that is, the word of faith that we proclaim); because, if you confess with your mouth that Jesus is Lord and believe in your heart that God raised him from the dead, you will be saved. For with the heart one believes and is justified, and with the mouth one confesses and is saved. ESV

Why, then, is resisting demonic oppression often so difficult? The answer lies in the layers of spiritual bondage that are inherited and embedded within culture, family, and personal behavior. Many struggle under the weight of generational, territorial, or bloodline curses. These inherited patterns, when left unchallenged, form belief systems that normalize sin. If a grandfather sinned, and then the father, uncles, and neighbors followed suit, the behavior begins to seem acceptable. This is how sin passes down and becomes a generational curse.

These inherited patterns are commonly known as generational curses. They are recurring cycles of dysfunction and rebellion that pass through bloodlines, distorting the perception of what is right and wrong. Then there are territorial sins—culturally ingrained behaviors that society may practice in secret but widely accepts or even celebrates. These are acts performed in darkness but spoken of as light. Despite clear opposition from Scripture and the church, people continue to embrace them, rebelling against God's truth.

In such cases, demonic influence may be at work. However, it is crucial to understand that not every instance of sin is due to demonic oppression. Sometimes, the issue is simply the flesh. Some individuals have the strength to resist temptation but choose not to exercise it. They are not necessarily bound by demonic power; they enjoy their sin and are unwilling to surrender it. In these moments, the devil receives undue credit for sins born from human willfulness and rebellion.

Ultimately, we must recognize that humanity plays a role in its bondage. Yes, there is a devil who tempts, but there is also a person who chooses. And it is that choice of one's will—that determines whether to walk in the darkness or the light.

These behavioral patterns are so deeply ingrained in the culture that when I traveled to a country in Latin America to sell computers wholesale, one client explained that in his store, most customers would purchase two computers: one for their household, and another for the home of their lover.

I will elaborate on this issue at greater length in a later chapter. But for now, understand this: the root of the problem remains Satan's relentless determination to "rob, kill, and destroy." He accomplishes this by corrupting everything related to man's purpose and destiny in the Kingdom of God, including families, ministries, and individual callings. His sole purpose for existing is driven by an insatiable desire for dominion and to perpetuate his influence across generations.

The question you may be asking yourself, dear reader, is this: how does Satan maintain such formidable power throughout the ages? Several factors contribute to his influence:

1. As I shared earlier, he is a spiritual being who was cast out of heaven and, therefore, had to devise a strategy to function on earth. He did so by organizing an army of fallen angels—demons—into a structured hierarchy operating at different levels of authority. This organized system includes principalities, powers, and rulers who govern various aspects of life across regions. Satan stands at the apex of this hierarchy, with spiritual forces operating beneath him in coordinated efforts to carry out his objectives.

Ephesians 6:11-12

Put on the whole armor of God, that ye may be able to stand against the wiles of the devil. For we wrestle not against flesh and blood, but against principalities, against powers, against the rulers of the darkness of this world, against spiritual wickedness in high places.

2. Satan's influence over a Christian does not imply possession. In fact, for those who are in Christ, possession is not possible, because they have been marked as God's own in baptism and indwelling by the Holy Spirit (2 Corinthians 1:22; Ephesians 1:13). However, spiritual oppression is real. The devil and his demons seek to deceive, accuse, and tempt believers with such intensity that their behavior may appear out of character, driven by fear, compulsion, or deep shame. Oppression can look like intrusive thoughts, overwhelming

urges, emotional torment, and persistent temptation—especially when tied to unresolved trauma or patterns of unrepentant sin. Yet even in these dark moments, the Holy Spirit does not abandon the believer. He groans with us and for us (Romans 8:26), calling us again to Christ.

3. Possession takes place when a demon, an evil spiritual being, must inhabit and control a person to the extent that the individual's behavior aligns with the demon's purpose. This influence manifests in acting out of character, altered speech, episodes of supernatural strength, and an inability to resist sinful behavior, even when the person understands its destructive consequences and has the spiritual insight to resist. People under demonic oppression may engage in actions they know will damage their reputation, cause public exposure, or ruin their lives, yet they yield under the pressure.

Some people even report being unable to resist the Devil when they feel compelled to sin. Often, when these individuals come into contact with a Spirit-filled Christian—someone anointed by God—the demons within them react violently and irrationally, unable to bear the presence of divine authority.

II Timothy 3:4-6

Treacherous, reckless, swollen with conceit, lovers of pleasure rather than lovers of God, ⁵ having the appearance of godliness, but denying its power. Avoid such people. ⁶ For among them are those who creep into households and capture weak women, burdened with sins and led astray by various passions.

The demons' actions are dependent on their assignment. Each spirit has a distinct name and function corresponding to its role in affliction. These spirits often collaborate, forming a network of manipulation and control that gains strength in unity until the host is entirely consumed. When I speak of destruction, I mean emotional harm, physical suffering, shame, guilt, and paralyzing fear.

Satan is also known as "The Accuser." For instance, the spirit of sexual perversion often aligns with spirits of immorality, alcoholism, violence, and addiction. The Bible speaks of "legions" of demons—many operating together within a single person. A striking example of this appears in the account of Jesus' exorcism of the Gerasene demoniac.

Although Scripture emphasizes that everyone is accountable for their actions—since God has granted free will and empowers believers through the Holy Spirit—generational curses also play a crucial role in shaping behavior. Some people are raised in homes where following Jesus is modeled; others are conditioned to accept sin as normal, even admirable.

Further, early childhood experiences, especially sexual abuse or molestation, can open spiritual doors that allow demonic influence. The effects of such trauma are profound and long-lasting. Victims may develop sexual dysfunction, disturbances, or deviant behaviors in adulthood. The earlier the abuse begins and the longer it persists, the greater the emotional, psychological, and spiritual impact on the individual's identity. Children who are molested often grow into adults who struggle with sexual immorality, infidelity, pornography, and habitual masturbation, among other harmful patterns.

According to the Word of God, generational curses are the inherited consequences of unrepentant sins passed from one generation to the next. These curses are not automatically broken; these require intentional repentance, renunciation, and spiritual deliverance. When a person decides to turn away from sin, accept Christ, and sever ties with any ancestral covenants, they must plead the blood of Jesus Christ as a divine weapon used to break their power and dismantle the strongholds of sin.

It is critical to understand that God does not hold people responsible for their forefathers' sins. Satan does. He uses these transgressions to gain legal access and extend his influence over families. In upcoming chapters, we will learn the specific spiritual mechanisms that sustain patterns of sin (Chapter 2) and the path toward deliverance and freedom (Chapter 5).

Generational Curses Can Be Broken:

• The Bible provides avenues for breaking generational patterns through repentance, faith, and seeking God's grace.

• The blood of Jesus Christ is the key to overcoming sin and nullifying its lasting consequences (Galatians 3:13).

• Individuals have the power to reject inherited patterns and embrace a new legacy in Christ.

1) Satan also derives power from the existence and activation of spiritual altars—a topic that will be amply discussed in the following chapter.

As you may have come to realize, the spiritual realm is not a metaphor or religious abstraction. It is a reality we must acknowledge, understand, and confront. This has nothing to do with religious ceremonies or tradition. It is real. And it is happening here, now, in the same world you and I live in.

Prayer

"The word is near you, in your mouth and your heart" (that is, the word of faith that we proclaim); because, if you confess with your mouth that Jesus is Lord and believe in your heart that God raised him from the dead, you will be saved. For with the heart, one believes and is justified, and with the mouth one confesses and is saved." In the name of Jesus, I declare that the reader's confession of faith will break every yoke and give him ears to hear and eyes to see this truth." In Jesus' name. AMEN.

Chapter 2
The Mystery of Altars

2 Corinthians 13:14

"May the grace of the Lord Jesus Christ, and the love of God, and the fellowship of the Holy Spirit be with you."

This Trinitarian blessing acknowledges the three distinct yet unified persons of the Christian faith: the Father, the Son (Jesus Christ), and the Holy Spirit. All three persons have existed since the foundation of the earth. As God incarnate, Jesus embodies the fullest Reality of Truth and is seated at the Father's right hand. All power and authority have been bestowed upon Him by the Father. Scripture teaches that believers worship the Father, the Son, and the Holy Spirit—expressing this devotion through prayer, praise, gratitude, and actions that honor their unique roles while affirming their shared divinity.

In the Old Testament, there are numerous accounts of men building altars for God whenever they called upon the Lord's name to commemorate His deeds or promises. These altars served as tangible signs of worship and gratitude.

Philippians 4:20

Now unto God and our Father be glory forever and ever. Amen.

Genesis 35:1-7

God said to Jacob, "Arise, go up to Bethel and dwell there. Make an altar there to the God who appeared to you when you fled from your brother Esau." So Jacob said to his household and to all who were with him, "Put away the foreign gods that are among you and purify yourselves and change your garments. Then let us arise and go up to Bethel, so that I may make there an altar to the God who answers me in the day of my distress and has been with me wherever I have gone." So they gave to Jacob all the foreign gods that they had, and the rings that were in their ears. Jacob hid them under the terebinth tree that was near Shechem. And as they journeyed, a terror from God fell upon the cities that were around them, so that they did not pursue the sons of Jacob. And Jacob came to Luz (that is, Bethel), which is in the land of Canaan, he and all the people who were with him, and there he built an altar and called the place El-bethel, because there God had revealed himself to him when he fled from his brother.

Genesis 8:20-22

Then Noah built an altar to the LORD and took some of every clean animal and some of every clean bird and offered burnt offerings on the altar. And when the LORD smelled the pleasing aroma, the LORD said in his heart, "I will never again curse[a] the ground because of man, for the intention of man's heart is evil from his youth. Neither will I ever again strike down every living creature as I have done. While the earth remains, seedtime and harvest, cold and heat, summer and winter, day and night, shall not cease."

Throughout the entire book of Genesis, there is no record of altars being constructed for demonic purposes; rather, altars were consistently built to honor and worship God. Drawing on Apostle Joshua Selman's teachings regarding ***"How Demonic Altars Play into Sexual Immorality and Sin in general,"*** this chapter will explore three key themes about altars and how demonic forces distort Godly concepts such as human sexuality:

1. A Biblical understanding of what altars truly represent
2. The connection between altars and the dominion that Christians possess.
3. How to establish worship altars for Godly purposes and dismantle demonic altars

The King James Version of the Bible mentions the altar 364 times. Today, however, many people associate altars with evil, superstition, or paganism. Yet, the concept of altars originates entirely from God, not the Devil. The word "altar" appears seven times in the book of Genesis in the King James Version. The first instance is in Genesis 8:20, where Noah builds an altar to God after the flood. Subsequent mentions occur in Genesis 12:7-8, 13:18, 22:9, 26:25, 33:20, and 35:14, referring to altars built by Abraham and Jacob.

What is an Altar?

1. An altar is a place, platform, or system where the spirit realm intersects with the physical realm on legal grounds. *(Luke 1:10-11)*

2. An altar serves as a platform that authorizes or permits laws or spirits to operate upon the earth. It is unlawful for spirits to function in the earthly realm without a legitimate body. Without a body, there is no rightful authority to act on earth. Furthermore, this body must possess a mind, a will, and an intellect to sustain that authority. This eliminates the possibility of possession of animal bodies for dominion purposes.

3. An altar is the foundational platform where covenants are established and maintained.

Many of us have become victims of altars, which explains why we might pray and fast over certain issues, yet see no breakthrough. Such situations can even make Jesus appear powerless. However, it requires knowledge as a godly believer to produce tangible results. Altars manifest not only as physical monuments or institutions but also as individuals or non-material, spiritual platforms. Despite their intangible nature, they are real and exert influence. The early church's patriots commanded remarkable dominion because they understood the mystery of altars. Altars enable all kinds of spirits to express themselves among humankind.

An individual can fall prey to negative or demonic altars, whether in churches, nations, businesses, or corporations. All can be affected. The primary function of an altar is to provide authorization and continuity to any spiritual activity, whether good or evil, godly or demonic.

Whenever God made promises or covenants with men, an altar was erected as a tangible sign of worship and gratitude. You can discern the presence of an altar in any life, family, or region by observing recurring patterns and events, whether positive or negative. If certain things consistently occur within a family, community, or an individual's life, it is an indication that an altar is sustaining either the good or the evil that is present.

For instance, the salvation of mankind is powered by an altar. It is on this very throne that God sits. Without the altar as a source of power or connection, salvation would be impossible.

Another example is the enduring altar of Israel. The Israelites are a people bound by a covenant with God and linked to an altar. This connection grants them an inexplicable advantage. Regardless of distance, location, era, age, or gender, the altar's influence persists. Even if the person who originally established the altar has passed away, the altar's authority remains in effect. If one believes in the message—and the altar tied to that message—it will function without fail.

Examples of Negative Altars:

1. All forms of addictions—drugs, alcohol, sex.

2. Mysterious diseases and infirmities—whether familial, individual, or territorial—are often passed down through the bloodline.

3. Various sexual and immoral perversions.

4. Depression and mental health struggles—these often require more than counseling because the root problem is sustained by the presence of an altar.

5. Witchcraft and idolatry. Even sincere Christians who love God sometimes unknowingly seek foundations of idolatry and feel comfortable seeking them out, no matter how much they know. This is because idolatry is empowered by demonic altars.

6. Stagnation and delay in life's progress.

7. Near-success syndrome—where people come close to success but never fully attain it.

8. Barrenness and short-lived victories—enjoying blessings that never endure.

9. Some pastors and families also become victims of altars.

10. All negative behavioral patterns are sustained by altars, whether we admit it or not.

Associations can also influence you to partake in or support certain behaviors, because the spiritual realm opposes some and favors others.

In America, an altar was raised for God, and the people called on the name of the Lord. That altar's voice continues to speak, as altars transcend time and remain effective beyond temporal limits.

Altars can affect individuals and families. Likewise, authentic altars support missionaries through prayer; these altars are sustained by devoted prayers and worship.

Galatians 3:13

Christ redeemed us from the curse of the law by becoming a curse for us—for it is written, "Cursed is everyone who is hanged on a tree".

How Altars Work

The measure of the spiritual authority and results attained by our fathers of faith was founded on altars. These were men and women who worshiped, prayed, and trusted deeply in God. Through these actions, spiritual altars were established that sustained and empowered their walk with the Lord. Conversely, all satanic altars derive their power from one primary altar—the altar of sin and iniquity. This functions as a system of authorization and communication, providing and maintaining a gateway for all evil in the sight of the Lord.

Judges 6:1

And the children of Israel did evil in the sight of the LORD: and the LORD delivered them into the hand of Midian seven years.

Sin operates at different levels: personal, territorial, and generationally linked to the bloodline curses discussed in chapter 1.

Hosea 7:1

"When I was healing Israel, Ephraim's sin was uncovered, along with Samaria's wickedness. While they craft lying schemes, the thief invades, and the gang of thieves plunders outside.

Romans 5:12-14

Just as sin entered the world through one man, and death resulted from sin, therefore everyone dies, because everyone has sinned. Certainly, sin was in the world before the Law was given, but no record of sin is kept when there is no law. Nevertheless, death ruled from the time of Adam to Moses, even over those who did not sin in the same way Adam did when he disobeyed. He is a foreshadowing of the one who would come.

John 9:1-2

As he was walking along, he observed a man who had been blind from birth. His disciples asked him, "Rabbi, who sinned, this man or his parents, that caused him to be born blind?

There are three levels of sin relevant to the operation of evil altars:

1. Personal sin – As 1 John 1:8 reminds us. If we claim to be without sin, we deceive ourselves and are not truthful.

2. Territorial sins – In Genesis 18:20-23, the LORD said, *"How great is the disapproval of Sodom and*

Gomorrah! Their sin is so very serious! I'm going down to see whether they've acted according to the protests that have reached me. If not, I wish to know. Then two of the men turned away from there and walked toward Sodom, while Abraham remained standing in the presence of the LORD. Abraham approached and asked, "Will you destroy the righteous along with the wicked?

3. Sin rooted in foundations, ancestry, and bloodlines – Jonah 1:1 Now this message from the LORD came to Amittai's son Jonah: Get up and go to Nineveh, that great city! Then cry out in protest against it, because their evil has come to my attention.

Psalm 11:3

When the foundations are destroyed, what can the righteous do?

Everyone is a victim of territorial sin. This sinfulness becomes embedded in our countries of origin and cultures to the point that it is normalized. People grow accustomed to seeing sinful behaviors as ordinary simply because 'everyone does it.' God did not remove the sinful nature from man because He granted us free will to choose good or evil. Along with this, He provided a moral compass and conscience to guide our decisions toward righteousness or otherwise. Redemption, procured through the sacrificial death of the Lamb on the cross, enables forgiveness of our sins.

Just as all evil altars are powered by sin, all godly altars derive their power from one supreme altar: The *Throne of Grace*. This is God's presence, a place where believers receive mercy and grace, particularly through Jesus Christ as our High Priest. The *Throne of Grace* fuels every good aspect of the believer's life, every system of exchange, interaction, and command for blessings.

Hebrews 4:14-6

Therefore, since we have a great high priest who has gone to heaven, Jesus the Son of God, let us live our lives consistent with our confession of faith. For we do not have a high priest who is unable to sympathize with our weaknesses. Instead, we have one who in every respect has been tempted as we are, yet he never sinned. So let us keep on coming boldly to the throne of grace, so that we may obtain mercy and find grace to help us in our time of need.
International Standard Version

Hebrews 12:22-24

But you have come right up into Mount Zion, to the city of the living God, the heavenly Jerusalem, and to the gathering of countless happy angels; and to the church, composed of all those registered in heaven; and to God who is Judge of all; and to the spirits of the redeemed in heaven, already made perfect; and to Jesus himself, who has brought us his wonderful new agreement; and to the sprinkled blood, which graciously forgives instead of crying out for vengeance as the blood of Abel did.
Living Bible version

Every believer should experience divine encounters and walk continuously in the grace of God at an altar, but the supreme altar is the *Throne of Grace*. The altars that truly ensure the fulfillment of God's promises are those rooted in the *Throne of Grace* — the source that empowers worship, prayer, favor, and blessings.

Hebrews 13:20-21

Now the God of peace, that brought again from the dead our Lord Jesus, that great shepherd of the sheep, through the blood of the everlasting covenant Make you perfect in every good work to do his will, working in you that which is well pleasing in his sight, through Jesus Christ; to whom be glory for ever and ever. Amen.

This truth is very powerful because, as Christians, we must align ourselves with the covenant of the altar. The moment we connect to that altar, we are united with the *Throne of Grace* itself.

How to Raise And Maintain Altars

Every man you see who is a champion in ministry demonstrates the undeniable results of consistently raised altars. In our time, believers may not erect physical structures as altars; however, dedicating a prayer room as an altar is still considered meaningful. However, altars are primarily erected within men's hearts because God looks beyond outward appearances—He sees the heart. When an individual chooses to raise an altar in his heart, he is empowered by the Holy Spirit to resist the devil, overcome temptations, reject sinfulness, and deny the allurements of the world. While Christians live in the world, we are not of the world. These spiritual altars remain vigilant even when we sleep and continue to operate regardless of our physical presence.

Elijah stands as a great patriarch who erected a mighty altar; he notably repaired the broken altar of the Lord (refer to 1 Kings 18:19-29 and 30–39).

1. Elijah repaired the broken altar, which represented a sacred place of repentance and brokenness. An altar cannot—and will not—be raised, maintained, or restored without genuine repentance and brokenness before the Lord. If we desire the power of God to manifest anew, we must begin with heartfelt brokenness and sincere repentance. It is not prophecy, offerings, or any other activity that initiates this; only true repentance and brokenness suffice (see 2 Samuel 24:1, 10–15). Fathers bear a solemn responsibility to intercede for the sins of their children and family members, pleading for mercy on their behalf. Without mercy, blessings from God cannot flow.

2. Elijah set up twelve stones in accordance with God's Word. Another essential component of an altar is the Word of God itself—the promises of God—alongside worship, sacrifice, prayers, praise, and the wholehearted commitment of the believer.

3. Sacrifice — There are five levels of sacrifice.

1. Myself – I present a conscious decision to belong to Him.

Romans 12:1

I beseech you therefore, brethren, by the mercies of God, that ye present your bodies a living sacrifice, holy, acceptable unto God, which is your reasonable service.

2. Our praise and worship

Hebrews 13:15

By him, therefore, let us offer the sacrifice of praise to God continually, that is, the fruit of our lips giving thanks to his name. Offer the sacrifice of praise, the fruit of our lips, giving thanks to his name.

3. Prayer – A major sacrifice.

Leviticus 6:13 declares that the fire shall ever be burning upon the altar; it shall never go out. This altar is none other than the altar of our hearts.

4. Sacrifice of seed and giving.

There must be a clear understanding, for seeds carry different voices within the realm of the spirit.

5. Prophetic decrees and blessings

1 Kings 18:33

And he put the wood in order, and cut the bullock in pieces, and laid him on the wood, and said, 'Fill four barrels with water, and pour it on the burnt sacrifice, and on the wood.' The sacrifice was in place, and he began calling on the God of Heaven.

Many ministers and businesspeople embark on ventures—whether it be churches, projects, businesses, relationships, marriages, or travels—without first establishing an altar or comprehending the benefits and powerful principles that altars represent. These altars are not physical monuments but rather intangible monuments of trust and faith in God's blessings and mercy. People often attempt to serve both God and Satan simultaneously, a contradiction that causes significant problems for them. They consult mediums and make pledges as misguided tokens, unaware of the gravity of their actions. The mystery of the altar is the mystery of dominion.

It is time to rise as priests, wielding wisdom's resources—among them, an understanding of altars. Whatever it takes, let us commit to being priests. The greatest harm we can inflict is passing down curses and a lack of understanding of altars to our children.

How to Tear Down Altars

To dismantle an altar of sin, begin by pleading for mercy over every evil altar. An evil altar is the source of power behind all that is dysfunctional and doesn't work. Begin by identifying any existing altars and pray in genuine repentance, not as a means of condemnation, but as a sincere confession to seek forgiveness on behalf of children, spouses, yourself, congregations, and any businesses or ministries involved.

Stagnation, delay, and sin persist because of altars that must be torn down and replaced with altars dedicated to the Lord if you desire transformation and a change of heart.

A broken and contrite heart, O God, you will not despise. This was King David's heartfelt plea for forgiveness when he sinned.

Psalm 51

Have mercy on me,[a] O God, according to your steadfast love; according to your abundant mercy
blot out my transgressions. Wash me thoroughly from my iniquity, and cleanse me from my sin! For I know my transgressions, and my sin is ever before me.
Against you, you only, have I sinned and done what is evil in your sight, so that you may be justified in your words and blameless in your judgment. Behold, I was brought forth in iniquity, and in sin did my mother conceive me. Behold, you delight in truth in the inward being, and you teach me wisdom in the secret heart. Purge me with hyssop, and I shall be clean;

wash me, and I shall be whiter than snow. Let me hear joy and gladness; let the bones that you have broken rejoice. Hide your face from my sins, and blot out all my iniquities. Create in me a clean heart, O God, and renew a right[b] spirit within me. Cast me not away from your presence, and take not your Holy Spirit from me. Restore to me the joy of your salvation, and uphold me with a willing spirit. Then I will teach transgressors your ways, and sinners will return to you. Deliver me from blood guiltiness, O God, O God of my salvation, and my tongue will sing aloud of your righteousness. O Lord, open my lips,

and my mouth will declare your praise. For you will not delight in sacrifice, or I would give it; you will not be pleased with a burnt offering. The sacrifices of God are a broken spirit; a broken and contrite heart, O God, you will not despise. Do good to Zion in your good pleasure; build up the walls of Jerusalem; then will you delight in right sacrifices, in burnt offerings and whole burnt offerings; then bulls will be offered on your altar.

We must connect destiny and glory to the altar called The *Throne of Grace*—not to ancestry, witchcraft, human manipulation, or any earthly platform. Our connection is to the *Throne of Grace*. My destiny, my glory, my work, my ministry, and the workings of the Spirit in my life are all anchored to the *Throne of Grace*, upheld by the God of the eternal covenant.

Let it be known to principalities and powers that a shift in loyalty has taken place—from the kingdom of darkness to the *Throne of Grace*. It is now God whom you obey, serve, and worship. Everyone is destined for greatness; the key is to be righteous before the Lord, your God. I will not fear the multitude of ten thousand who set themselves against me. I lay myself down and wait for the Lord to take me and transform me.

Any system of authorization rooted in personal sin, bloodline iniquity, or territorial sin must be completely broken. Every negative pattern that contradicts the Word of God must be utterly destroyed. Delay, limitation, sickness, death, poverty, begging, and hardship—these must be shattered immediately. Inferiority and mediocrity, be broken now in the name of Jesus. Rise to the fullness of God's design without delay.

I command my destiny and priesthood to open wide. I enter into the realm of prosperity and shut the gates of the spirit realm against anything targeting me, my family, my ministry, or my business associates. I break every spiritual grounding in my life now. I shut off the power of the sun, the wind, and every medium of expression; no one shall ever again respond to or serve the enemy.

A sacrifice is not merely an offering of money; it is a spiritual ordinance in favor of my destiny. An opportunity to offer a sacrifice is not about making a donation; it marks the ending of one season and the beginning of another.

I declare the Word and acknowledge that seeds bear fruit according to the integrity of God's word, bloodlines, and foundations. We are committed to the one true God. We are about to lay down sacrifices, repent of our sins, and cry out through our spiritual priesthood. May fire fall upon your sacrifice—may fire fall upon your sacrifice. Every demonic spirit witnesses the sacrifice and all that it entails. I declare that the heavens open over every issue needing to be presented to the Lord. For all that has refused to work in my life, I decree that every door swings wide open in the name of Jesus. Father, I stand firm in the privilege of priesthood and the body of Christ by the election of grace.

There is power in covenants. God is a God of covenants, and He is in covenant with His children—the children of the Kingdom of God—through the blood of the Lamb. This blood covenant sustains believers' loyalty to Jesus Christ, their faith, and their commitment to serve Him alone.

The devil, although an imitator, never enters into covenants because he is the Father of Lies and would break every promise. Instead, he actively commands his power to influence and tempt people to sin, doing so persistently. He does not appear as a devil dressed in red with a fork in hand. He often appears as a seductive woman to tempt those vulnerable to sexual immorality, or as a friend enticing another to indulge in drugs, alcohol, or crime. Believe it or not, he wields power over the world and those who disobey God.

1 Corinthians 6:18-20

Flee from sexual immorality. Every other sin a person commits is outside the body, but the sexually immoral person sins against his own body. Or do you not know that your body is a temple of the Holy Spirit within you, whom you have from God? You are not your own, for you were bought with a price. So glorify God in your body.

Examples of sexual immorality and sinful altars sustained and perpetuated in today's society:

The Catholic Church's handling of sexual abuse cases, including cover-ups and prioritizing institutional interests over victims, perpetuates the sin. This functions as a system—or altar—that shields perpetrators rather than confronting abuse, maintaining a culture of secrecy and denial.

How do churches deal with sin and scandal? Approaches vary widely. Some seem indifferent to sin and scandal, depending on who is involved. Others permit ministers who commit adultery to continue preaching hellfire and brimstone on Sundays. Still others dismiss scandals involving church leaders as "between them and God," urging the congregation to mind their own business. Other churches, of course, will take appropriate measures by removing the minister from their assignments to counsel and deliver them from their areas of sinfulness and weakness, sometimes effectively and at times, ineffectively.

How does God deal with sexual immorality? Though merciful, He addresses it personally. The Holy Spirit will talk to the sinner's heart, prompt him or her to change their behavior, and mend their ways. He will keep it private, giving the person the opportunity to change. God keeps this private to allow for transformation, but when the Godly calls are ignored, he will be left without recourse, making it public and shaming the person, but only as a last resort.

Prayer

May fire fall upon your sacrifice and set you free of every demonic oppression as you build an altar of righteousness. May your repentance and the blood of Jesus speak justice and deliverance from every demonic spirit and oppression. I declare that the heavens open over every sin presented before the Lord, and I decree that every door swings wide open in the name of Jesus. Father, I stand firm in the privilege of priesthood and the body of Christ by the election of grace, in THE NAME OF JESUS. AMEN.

Chapter 3
Deliverance from Sexual Immorality

Breaking Out of Sexual Addictions

More people struggle with issues surrounding sexual addiction than we could ever imagine. The goal of this chapter is not to bring condemnation or to promote a sense of guilt, shame, or fear, but rather to equip readers with spiritual tools—insight, biblical principles, and practical steps. The goal is to assist those affected to overcome this deeply rooted issue. To discover God's plan for purity and the transformative power of His grace to break the chains of addiction. This message offers hope, healing, and empowerment for those wrestling with sexual sin. Additionally, it provides insight and valuable wisdom for counselors, pastors, spouses, or anyone supporting loved ones battling addictions. May this teaching serve as a pathway to freedom in Christ from sexual immorality and all related perversions and addictions.

1 Thessalonians 4:3-5

For this is the will of God, that you be sanctified [separated and set apart from sin]: that you abstain and back away from sexual immorality; that each of you know how to control his own body in holiness and honor [being available for God's purpose and separated from things profane], not [to be used] in lustful passion, like the

Gentiles who do not know God and are ignorant of His will. — Amplified Bible

Acts 15:28-29

For it seemed good to the Holy Spirit and us not to place on you any greater burden than these essentials: that you abstain from things sacrificed to idols, and from [consuming] blood, and from [eating the meat of] things that have been strangled, and from sexual impurity. If you keep yourselves from these things, you will do well. Farewell. — Amplified Bible

In this chapter, I will again draw on Apostle Joshua Selman's teachings on breaking free from sexual addictions to deepen our understanding of the complex and perplexing sin of sexual immorality and its many dire consequences. Sexual immorality is entrenched in society and extends to all individuals and organizations alike.

Apostle Guillermo Maldonado puts it this way: If a man or woman deliberately dwells on or imagines a scenario to the extent that they vividly visualize committing adultery with a particular person, and the emotion of sexual desire fully awakens, they have already sinned—even if the act was never physically committed. Sexual fantasies, imaginations, or voluntary meditations on such acts constitute the sin of sexual immorality in the heart. Jesus articulated this principle clearly: sin begins with the planting of a seed in the mind as a mere thought. If this thought is not rejected, the seed takes root and grows, eventually producing a harvest in the form of dire consequences of sin.

Sexual desire versus sexual immorality is predicated on facts you must know.

The desire for intimacy is not demonic. That is the problem with this issue of lust and immorality. While both are sins, sexual desire differs fundamentally from sins such as lying or stealing because the sexual drive was intentionally placed within us by God, not the devil. This desire cannot simply be cast out of your life. It is a God-ordained longing designed to be expressed under specific conditions; whether the expression is right or wrong depends on the presence or absence of those conditions, not on the desire itself. What makes it dangerous is that sexual desire can be one of the greatest blessings within marriage, for it is God who created the desire for intimacy in men. If you fail to grasp this, you risk becoming embroiled in a battle you cannot understand or win.

The spirit of lust and immorality exploits the blessing God instilled in men, twisting it into a destructive force against its victims. Sexual immorality is indiscriminate, and it cares not whether you are young or old, an apostle or a prophet, righteous or flawed. This issue transcends the binary of good and evil; it involves the exploitation not of weakness but of a God-given provision. Without proper guardianship of one's sexuality, grounded in Godly teachings, even a person of noble character can fall victim. Sexual immorality is a corrosive cancer that has destroyed individuals, ministries, businesses, political careers, and noble destinies—sometimes overnight.

No man will ever outgrow the temptation of sexual intimacy because it is a desire that is innate to man and planted by God Himself. The devil will come over and over again as long as you are alive because he knows that desire is present in every man. He will create scenarios to make men or women fall because that nature is present in everyone. When one is ignorant and not equipped with the Scripture and revelation, one will eventually become a victim.

In the context of spiritual immorality, I have come to understand that, while it possesses carnal elements, its root is spiritual in nature. For the young and unmarried, the spirit of lust intensifies God's original desire beyond natural control. This amplification is driven by a spirit opposed to God, one that magnifies the longing to an overwhelming degree (I acknowledge, but will not discuss here, the role of hormones and physical factors). Generally, this spirit magnifies desire until it becomes uncontrollable, then, paradoxically, upon marriage, it often diminishes drastically, as if it evaporated. This shift reflects the destructive influence of the spirit.

Beyond sexual immorality itself, there are other expressions, such as pornography, masturbation, and various perversions, which depend on several conditions: 1) They are atmosphere-dependent; 2) They require mutual consent between parties, except in cases of pornography and masturbation. Some individuals may survive sexual immorality but succumb to these other disorderly vices. Certain acts are not physically enacted but represent ongoing emotional indulgence; yet, according to God, the sin is already committed. Regardless of your status, whether man of God, single, married, young, old, or in ministry, if left unchecked, these practices will attack and destroy your life.

There are other expressions of immorality, such as drunkenness and drug abuse, closely related to perversions like pornography and masturbation. Sexual immorality often requires the presence of other enabling conditions, such as intoxication, substance abuse, distorted imaginations, or bodily harm inconsistent with God's design. More severe acts—such as sexual abuse of children, bestiality, sodomy, and rape—are equally egregious and wholly contrary to God's pattern.

As indicated at the beginning of this chapter, the goal is not condemnation; rather, it is to expose the devil's role in this struggle and bring conviction to the heart, so that true freedom can be attained. Many desire deliverance but lack understanding of the process involved. Therefore, I present five scriptural steps that will liberate you from sexual immorality and other perversions. Please take these to heart, for these five steps can break the enemy's grasp on your life and set you free to enjoy the God-given gift of sexuality fully.

1. To be free from sexual immorality, you must first acknowledge your need for help.

Freedom from lust, immorality, and any manifestation thereof begins with honest admission. You must come with a broken spirit and a repentant heart to keep your salvation. This acknowledgement should be deeply contemplated until you reach the point of genuine confession. Many suffer under sexual sin; on closer examination, we find that while they know it is wrong, they remain trapped by this stronghold. They have a sincere desire to be free but have yet to break the chains of bondage. Often, this struggle is rooted in cultural influences. Perhaps these sins were normalized within families or even endorsed as common practice. Some communities even integrate such behaviors into their cultural activities. Always approach those caught in these snares with compassion and mercy. Remember, the first step toward freedom is the honest admission of your need for deliverance. Any hidden weakness left unconfessed will ultimately bring you down.

Psalm 51:1

Have mercy on me, O God, according to Your lovingkindness;
According to the greatness of Your compassion, blot out my transgressions.
Wash me thoroughly from my wickedness and guilt And cleanse me from my sin. For I am conscious of my transgressions and I acknowledge them; My sin is always before me. Against You, You only, have I sinned And done that which is evil in Your sight, So that You are justified when You speak [Your sentence] And faultless in Your judgment. I was brought forth in [a state of] wickedness; In sin my mother conceived me [and from my beginning I, too, was sinful]. Behold, You desire truth in the innermost being, And in the hidden part [of my heart] You will make me know wisdom. Purify me with [a]hyssop, and I will be

clean; Wash me, and I will be whiter than snow. Make me hear joy and gladness and be satisfied; Let the bones which You have broken rejoice. Hide Your face from my sins And blot out all my iniquities. Create in me a clean heart, O God, And renew a right and steadfast spirit within me. Do not cast me away from Your presence And do not take Your Holy Spirit from me. Restore to me the joy of Your salvation And sustain me with a willing spirit. Then I will teach transgressors Your ways, And sinners shall be converted and return to You.

Rescue me from blood guiltiness, O God, the God of my salvation; Then my tongue will sing joyfully of Your righteousness and Your justice. O Lord, open my lips, that my mouth may declare Your praise. For you do not delight in sacrifice, or else I would give it; You are not pleased with burnt offering. My [only] sacrifice [acceptable] to God is a broken spirit; A broken and contrite heart [broken with sorrow for sin, thoroughly penitent], such, O God, You will not despise. By Your favor, do good to Zion; May You rebuild the walls of Jerusalem. Then will You delight in the sacrifices of righteousness, In burnt offering and whole burnt offering; Then young bulls will be offered on Your altar.

2. Set aside time for an honest repentance retreat.

A retreat offers a dedicated space for prayer, heartfelt brokenness, and sincere repentance before your Maker. It provides the necessary time to fast and deeply study the Scriptures concerning these matters. You cannot afford to be too busy, because neglecting to confront this issue will ultimately destroy you. When facing something as corrosive as this spiritual cancer, you must intentionally set aside time for a retreat. In the demonic assignment of sexual immorality, it is not merely the act of sex that destroys; rather, it is living in denial—assuming no problem exists—that brings ruin. This affliction is designed to destroy you spiritually first, then physically. The devil attacks and possesses you, introducing this bondage in a way that opens the door for assaults in every dimension of your life. There is a strong relationship between spiritual immorality and untimely death. The enemy's purpose is your destruction—know this truth deeply.

Immerse yourself in the entirety of Psalm 51, the Psalm of mercy and repentance. This spirit can lie dormant within you for years, patiently waiting for moments of pride and exaltation to topple you, one scandal after another. Recognize your need for help and actively seek to secure the power of God on your side. These demonic patterns are powerful and relentless. Whether you are a leader, a pastor, a husband, a father, or anyone else, the spirit rooted in your ancestry will hunt you until you employ spiritual intelligence to overcome it, or it will consume you. Never assume you are fine; if you have been exposed to these conditions, falling is inevitable. It is only a matter of time.

3. Be honest enough to seek help from mature people who can handle these issues.

History shows that often men of God fail to maintain the necessary spiritual intelligence and maturity because the church, or the counselor, is ill-equipped to address these issues appropriately. They betray the trust of those struggling, and that trust must be fiercely protected. Genuine help is powerful. It is remarkable how seemingly insurmountable mountains can be moved in the presence of authentic help and God's presence. Those battling these strongholds carry curses and evil spirits that mere counseling cannot resolve. You may find yourself counseling afflicted individuals, but the spirit waits at the counselor's door, ready to regroup and overwhelm the person the moment they leave the counselor's office. That is why individuals caught in sexual immorality or addiction remain silent during conversations. When asked, "Will you do this again?" they say no, yet by evening, they succumb once more. Do you understand how this spirit operates? Even when they are in unfamiliar surroundings, this spirit coordinates pathways to know where to find substances, whom to approach, and how to attack. It is a singular spirit or a coalition of many, but unless addressed decisively, the attacks intensify, and the problems escalate.

4. Create rules and boundaries in and around your life and be accountable to someone you trust.

Proverbs 25:28

Many people avoid or ignore this crucial step, which is why deliverance often remains incomplete. Do not allow your emotions to dictate your boundaries. This is how it must be. Repentance and renewed resolve alone are insufficient; systems and safeguards must be deliberately established, especially regarding sexual immorality. Sexual immorality is highly influenced by environmental and atmospheric factors. Just as it is done with substance abuse and alcoholism, have a person you can call at any time of day or night and be accountable to them.

5. Connect to a larger family of believers.

Hebrews 10:25

"Not forsaking our meeting together [as believers for worship and instruction], as is the habit of some, but encouraging one another; and all the more [faithfully] as you see the day [of Christ's return] approaching."
Living within a community of believers is essential to sustaining kingdom values.

Review:

1. Admit there is a need for help.
2. Set aside time for a retreat.
3. Seek help from mature individuals capable of handling these issues.
4. Establish clear rules and boundaries in your life.
5. Connect with a larger family of believers.

Prayer

Father, I voluntarily change alliances to no longer serve the devil and his demonic enticements. As of today, I commit to serving Jesus Christ, my lord and Savior. With all my soul, I cry out to You for deliverance as I repent of all my sins. I choose this day to come out of agreement with the spirit of lust and command it, "Lust, get out of my soul now in the name of Jesus Christ!" Lord, Jesus, save me and cleanse me from all unrighteousness and make me as white as snow that I may glorify You with my life. Wash me in Your Blood, I plead mercy, justice, and righteousness. Create in me a clean heart and renew a right spirit within me, Oh Lord. Father, I thank You for saving me and delivering me from this sinfulness! Let the Kingdom of God come into my life now in Jesus' Name. Amen!

Chapter 4
Reasons Christians Remain Trapped in Sexual Immorality

Christians, Ordained Ministers, Priests, and Sex Scandals

We have all watched—sometimes in disbelief and sorrow—as respected Christian leaders, preachers, and priests with thriving ministries fall into sexual sin, destroying all they have accomplished. We learn from the Bible that some causes of those falls are that some people, when they are spiritual "babes in Christ," do not understand the importance of discerning good and evil or the risks of not maturing in the faith with a sound foundation. In 1 Corinthians 3:1-2, the Apostle Paul addresses the Corinthians, saying he cannot speak to them as spiritual people, but rather as carnal—as infants in Christ. *"I fed you with milk, not solid food, for you were not yet able to receive it; no, not even now are you able.* Immature believers are particularly vulnerable to temptation, discouragement, and spiritual decline.

Others, while growing in the faith, resist surrendering fully to God. They continue to cling to worldly habits and fail to crucify the flesh. They fail to learn to resist the devil, to stand strong against the schemes of demonic activity, and sooner or later end up yielding to their fleshly and sinful nature. Galatians 5:17 tells us that the flesh strives against the Spirit and the Spirit against the flesh.*" Therefore, any attempt to battle sexual sin—or any sin—must be approached spiritually and biblically. It requires dying to the flesh by the power of the Cross and the assistance of the Holy Spirit.

When believers rely solely on human strength to resist sin, defeat is inevitable. Victory comes only by yielding to the power of the Holy Spirit. The flesh loves all the world has to offer, all that is carnal, selfish, ego-centric, and ungodly. The carnal man loves these things so much that he does not stop to think what they are exposing themselves to. Yet the dangers are very real: sexually transmitted diseases, spiritual contamination, the formation of ungodly soul ties, broken marriages, disqualified ministries, and ultimately, a tragic fall from grace.

The flesh cannot be rehabilitated, reasoned with, or reformed. It operates by a law of self-centeredness. It demands its way and lives to gratify its desires. This "old self"—the sinful nature—is driven by emotion, lust, and pride, and must be put to death daily by the Spirit.

The Bible teaches us the order in which a new believer should grow:

1. **Salvation** – Confessing Jesus as Lord and Savior, accompanied by sincere repentance from sin.
2. **Transformation** – A lifelong, non-linear process of spiritual renewal, brought about by the study of the Word, active church participation, meaningful fellowship, a consistent prayer life, and a deepening relationship with God rooted in His unconditional love and truth.

3. Water Baptism – A symbolic act of cleansing and repentance, representing the burial of the old self and rising anew in Christ.

4. Baptism in the Holy Spirit – Empowerment through immersion in the Spirit, often evidenced by the gift of speaking in tongues.

5. Inner Healing – The recognition and healing of emotional wounds, traumas, and abuses that continue to hinder spiritual growth and maturity.

6. Deliverance – Freedom from demonic oppression, influences, and generational curses that cause the individual to be pressured into sin, delay spiritual growth, and remain an easy prey for evil spirits to oppress them further.

Though believers receive salvation by grace through faith, that same grace must also be exercised in claiming victory over the flesh and soul (carnal) life by the same grace, which is faith in the Lord Jesus Christ. It is not by works, big efforts, or prayers; it is a gift obtained through the confession of faith in Jesus Christ, who accepts us just as we are.

Spiritual growth is not a linear process; it takes several years for a believer to attain a degree of maturity in their godly character, enough that they can be allowed to actively participate in ministry through their spiritual gifts. Although no one can say that they have arrived or completely matured, that they have reached their goal, and know everything there is to learn. This is known as the arrival mentality and denotes more pride than maturity.

In the Kingdom of God, believers never stop learning all there is to know about the Kingdom of God, heaven and earth, His design for mankind, and the mysteries of eternity. However, some believers want to accelerate the transformation process by skipping steps because the process is long and treacherous. And because they skipped some steps through which a believer must be processed, they continue to carry the oppressions and curses discussed in this book thus far.

This explains why many ministers, pastors, priests, and Christian leaders are never delivered of evil spirits, who can and will catch up with them. Since their resistance to the demons is weak, they play a waiting game. The demons, cunning and patient, may even assist the man in his initial success, fully aware that his eventual fall is inevitable. They retreat into the shadows, acting as if they've disappeared, all the while biding their time.

Mark 16:16

> *Whoever believes and is baptized will be saved, but whoever does not believe will be condemned.*

Meanwhile, these unseen forces watch as the individual advances in rank, tempting them with sin. They work to convince him that his spiritual condition will remain hidden, that his sinful tendencies can be concealed indefinitely. But demons are strategic—they wait for just the right time, place, and season to bring about a dramatic and devastating fall. After all, the devil is known as *the accuser of the brethren*, and his tactics are rooted in exposure and shame.

Most importantly, while God is merciful, He cannot be mocked or defied. Every act of rebellion and every disregard for His commandments will, in due time, be brought to light sooner or later. His justice prevails as he is a God of Righteousness, the judge in Heaven's court.

Galatians 6:7 tells us that "God cannot be mocked."

Had this man been delivered—or had he even understood how demons operate to maintain influence or reclaim control over a person—he might have stood a chance against such a fall. But more often than not, individuals succumb to one or more of the major life destroyers: Sex, Power, and Money.

If you allow any of these three life destroyers to rule over you, the enemy will weaponize them to orchestrate your downfall. What follows is not just defeat but humiliation—public and painful. It's not a matter of *if* but *when.*

However, for the believer who is patient and perseveres, who is firm and faithful in their commitment to Jesus, change will come. It is certain to happen because Jesus Christ is faithful to His covenant and promises.

Whenever a person needs to confront sin, the first and most vital step is addressing the flesh—the sinful nature inherent in every human being. The work of the Holy Spirit, accomplished through the Cross, was dual, involving both death and resurrection. There can be no resurrection without death. What was true for the Lord must also be true for us, in our thoughts, our emotions, and our carnal desires.

The flesh must remain crucified, forever nailed to the Cross. But the mind must rise—resurrected into the renewed mind of Christ. This renewed mind seeks what He seeks, feels what He feels, and desires what He desires, as we are transformed by learning and obeying His Word.

Romans 12:2

And be not conformed to this world: but be ye transformed by the renewing of your mind, that ye may prove what is that good, and acceptable, and perfect, will of God.

A man without Jesus Christ and the leading of the Holy Spirit will always contend against the will of God. Just as we receive salvation by grace through faith, we must also claim victory over the flesh and soul-life by that same grace— through faith in Jesus Christ.

It is not a matter of effort or merit, but of trust. Victory is not earned by hard labor but gained by belief. It is essential to understand that God is on your side and that the Holy Spirit wants to heal every broken part of your life and to fulfill your deepest needs. Believe this truth in your heart— and declare it with your mouth!

One more important truth I want to interject at this point is the fact that a transference of spirits takes place when having sex with another person. To "transfer" a spirit means to transmit or convey an unseen spiritual force from one person to another. Something from their character, better described as an evil spirit, is transferred from one party to the other, and vice versa. We know evil spirits make the condition of each person in the equation harder to deal with and break free from. This exchange opens doors—entry points—for the enemy.

This deeply entrenched strategy of spirit transference accounts for a significant number of spiritual battles faced by both believers and non-believers. Tragically, many are unaware of this tactic, which explains sudden, dramatic shifts in behavior, often from good to evil, or from peace to unrest. In cases involving multiple sexual partners, the spiritual implications multiply exponentially.

The reader might be wondering why evil spirits would seek to transfer from one person to another during a sexual encounter, and not just to one partner, but to as many individuals as that person is sexually active with. A key reason Satan targets the human spirit is that it is through the spirit that communion with the Holy Spirit occurs. It is the spirit that bears witness to our salvation and confirms our identity as children of God: *"The Spirit itself bears witness with our spirit, that we are the children of God."* Romans 8:16 assures us that *"the Spirit himself testifies and confirms together with our spirit that we are children of God."* This truth is evident in the lives of holy men and women who revere their bodies, fully aware that they are *"temples of the Spirit of God."*

However, the Spirit of the Lord does not dwell in a person whose life is marked by unchecked promiscuity, where the temple has been desecrated and evil has gained entry. In such cases, the enemy seizes the opportunity to invade and oppress the soul.

Another foundational reason for this spiritual assault is that God uses the human spirit as a means of guidance and discernment. Just as a candle provides light and direction in the natural world, so too does the spirit provide illumination in the spiritual realm: *"The spirit of man is the candle of the Lord, searching all the inward parts of the belly."* Proverbs 20:27 reminds us that *"the spirit of man is the lamp of the Lord, searing and examining all the innermost parts of his being."*

Prayerfully, we hope that full surrender to the Holy Spirit's leading will be sufficient to break the chains of sexual immorality and other persistent sins. However, there are situations where the issue is not merely of the flesh—it may be rooted deeper, requiring additional spiritual strategies for deliverance. This often explains why the problem has been longstanding and follows a certain pattern of behavior. In such cases, the believer must seek insight and discernment from the Holy Spirit to identify the spiritual forces or foundational causes behind their oppression. Ordinarily, believers can exercise their will to overcome most temptations of the flesh. However, when that seems compromised—when it is "bound" and the individual is unable to break free or continually relapses into sin—then one must consider that darker forces may be at work. Deliverance may require more intentional intervention and spiritual warfare.

These obstacles could include demonic strongholds, generational curses, or entrenched altars of iniquity that maintain a grip on the sinner, refusing to release them without a struggle. In Chapter 1, I discussed how generational curses —whether personal, territorial, or rooted in bloodlines —are particularly difficult to break. In Chapter 2, I examined how spiritual altars perpetuate sin and unrighteousness. Dismantling these altars and building a new one within the spirit of man is critical. More precisely, it must be raised within the heart—an altar of worship, thanksgiving, praise, and adoration. It is there that one can humbly surrender their life and vulnerabilities, presenting themselves before the Throne of Grace to find mercy and help in their time of need.

Hebrews 4:16

Let us therefore come boldly unto the throne of grace, that we may obtain mercy, and find grace to help in time of need.

Once the heart is surrendered and the soul aligned, the process of renunciation must begin. Begin by breaking ties with generational curses that have operated throughout your life, starting with those rooted in your country of origin. These may include the spirits of poverty, religiosity, chronic illness, or sexual sin that runs through the family line.

For example, perhaps the grandfather had multiple women, illegitimate children, or experienced a broken marriage. Or maybe poverty, sickness, or alcoholism have persisted across generations. Look also at the behavior of your father, uncles, and aunts—on both maternal and paternal sides. Were there repeated cycles of broken relationships, divorces, children born of various partners, or long-term cohabitation without marriage? Find patterns and cycles and start renouncing with a repentant heart, asking for forgiveness from the Lord for the sinfulness and iniquity of the ancestors.

Besides the actual sexual encounters, there are other inordinate demonstrations of affection that must also be acknowledged and brought under spiritual discipline. These include unregulated, disorderly, and immoderate expressions of physical contact—whether with individuals of the same or opposite sex—that exceed appropriate relational boundaries. Such overt displays, when left unchecked, become excessive and dishonoring, not only to oneself but to God. Once we receive Christ as Savior, it becomes essential to reexamine the nature of our relationships through the lens of holiness. Every inappropriate activity, action, thought, desire, touch, and attitude should be confessed as sin and never be engaged again, no matter how much appreciation one has for the other. Boundaries are necessary. Oftentimes, it is important not only to be mindful of not sinning but also of not giving the appearance of sin.

Disorderly affections include unnaturally intimate friendships, emotional entanglements, or inappropriate physical contact, whether heterosexual or homosexual, as well as shared participation in other sinful behaviors. Salvation calls us to examine every relationship through the filter of God's Word, ensuring none violate His precepts.

Because the carnal mind is at enmity with God—unable and unwilling to submit to His authority; we must remain vigilant. Scripture warns us that evil companionships and corrupt associations inevitably damage our moral fabric and character. As it is written: *"If any man be in Christ, he is a new creature; old things have passed away; behold, all things have become new."*

God wants to put His Spirit—the Holy Spirit—within you so you can live for Him. This very truth is why Satan fiercely attacks our spirit: to hinder our surrender and sabotage our divine calling. He understands that it is only the man or woman with the right spirit whom God uses for Kingdom purposes. Satan is not an innovator—he is an imitator and a usurper, forever striving to counterfeit what God has already made perfect.

In view of the above, it would be safe to say that man's greatest weakness is ignorance. A lack of spiritual knowledge or understanding—specifically, revelation knowledge concerning how the enemy operates—is dangerous. Ignorance regarding the dynamics of how the spiritual and the physical realm interact to either stifle a person's growth and well-being or open the door to unrelenting defeat. The inability to discern how blessings or curses are activated across generations, territories, and bloodlines leaves one susceptible to attacks that could otherwise be prevented. To build a strategy for freedom—especially from sexual immorality or any deeply rooted sin—it is critical to connect the lessons in this chapter to the discussions in previous chapters concerning altars, generational iniquities, and spiritual strongholds.

John 8:36

"If the Son sets you free, you will be free indeed."

In Chapter 5, we will discuss deliverance as the ultimate response to free a believer who finds themselves spiritually bound—unable to surrender their will to Christ, unable to control their behavior and desires to sin, and has tried to stop practicing all the strategies previously suggested in this book. A believer cannot be possessed by demons, but can be influenced and oppressed to such a degree that they need to be delivered from demonic influence to set them free of oppression. The process, preparation, and conditions of the person being delivered, as well as the minister performing the delivery, will be discussed, as this is not a practice that can be taken lightly.

Prayer

Finally, my brethren, be strong in the Lord, and in the power of his might. Put on the whole armor of God, that ye may be able to stand against the wiles of the devil. For we wrestle not against flesh and blood, but against principalities, against powers, against the rulers of the darkness of this world, against spiritual wickedness in high places. Wherefore take unto you the whole armor of God, that ye may be able to withstand in the evil day, and having done all, to stand. Stand therefore, having your loins girt about with truth, and having on the breastplate of righteousness;

And your feet shod with the preparation of the gospel of peace; Above all, taking the shield of faith, wherewith ye shall be able to quench all the fiery darts of the wicked. And take the helmet of salvation, and the sword of the Spirit, which is the word of God: Praying always with all prayer and supplication in the Spirit and watching thereunto with all perseverance and supplication for all saints. —Ephesians 6:10 - 18

Chapter 5
Deliverance from Sexual Immorality
And all other Sins

I Thessalonians 5:23

And the very God of peace sanctify you wholly; and I pray God your whole spirit, and soul, and body be preserved blameless unto the coming of our Lord Jesus Christ.

What God Thinks About Sexual Sin

Scripture establishes in *1 Corinthians 6:18* that, *"every sin that a man does is without the body; but he that commits fornication sins against his own body."*

Furthermore, the Bible exhorts us not to engage in sensuality outside the bounds of marriage. It warns that the root of much conflict lies in *"your pleasures that wage war in your members"* (*James 4:1*, often mis-referenced as James 3:18). The Apostle Peter also warned that many would follow after sensuality, maligning the way of truth and yielding to the desires of the flesh (*2 Peter 2:2, 9–10, 18–21*).

By now, the reader will likely understand that within the Kingdom of God, there are both mysteries and rules of engagement—principles that must be learned, respected, and lived out. Some of these have already been revealed in this book. To bear fruit in the spiritual realm, we must walk with

Jesus Christ in integrity and upright character; otherwise, our growth as believers may be stunted or delayed.

Let me draw a parallel from the natural realm. Just as certain rules must be followed in the spiritual realm, the same applies in the physical if you are to survive in this world. For example, if you drive a car, you must know, understand, and adhere to traffic laws. Ignorance or disregard for these rules can lead to disastrous outcomes: accidents, license suspension, or harm to others. In the same way, spiritual ignorance or disobedience carries consequences that may not be immediately visible, but are no less real or severe.

Hebrews 11:3

By faith we understand that the worlds are framed by the word of God, so that the things which are seen were not made of things which are visible.

There is a supernatural world beyond this physical realm that has supremacy over the physical realm we know and understand. This invisible dimension is the origin of all that is visible. Nothing manifests in the natural realm unless it first exists in the spiritual realm. That which is not birthed in the spirit cannot take form in the physical.

There are, however, a few key challenges when it comes to engaging spiritual realities:

1. Many people ignore, overlook, or lack understanding of the spiritual realm altogether. This is a serious oversight, as God has made abundant spiritual resources available to every believer in Christ to bless them, to help them prosper, to protect them from danger, and to enjoy all that the Father has in store for His children.

2. People ignore how to engage those spiritual provisions or to profit from them in their material expressions. Nonetheless, in this chapter, I will focus on the matters that pertain to the dealings related to the deliverance of believers from the evil spirits (demons) that oppress them sexually or otherwise.

In this chapter, we will learn the deliverance process in three steps and how to practice self-deliverance:

1. The preparation of the believer to experience deliverance
2. The preparation of the deliverance minister
3. How to maintain the deliverance and be filled with the indwelling of the Holy Spirit
4. How to Practice Self-Deliverance

Let us begin by exploring some of the rules of engagement in the spiritual realm. Although the process of deliverance unfolds in the natural realm, where both the minister and the believer reside, it is deeply intertwined with the spiritual realm. After all, that is the origin of the demonic forces that come to possess, oppress, or influence an individual. It is also the realm to which they are returned once cast out. The spiritual realm is just as real as the demons expelled from individuals and sent back to that unseen dimension—to hang on the cross, awaiting judgment from the Judge of Heaven, and forbidden from returning to the person they once tormented or to anyone else.

That is, unless a door is reopened to them through acts of sinfulness.

Allow me to share two experiences from past deliverance sessions I conducted. These will help illustrate just how real—and how powerful—demonic forces can be. As I mentioned in the first chapter, demons are not only real but also highly organized, strategic, and deceptive, willing to go to extraordinary lengths to retain control over the people they inhabit.

Case No. 1:

Several years ago, I met with a woman who was scheduled for deliverance at the church where I attended. The session was set to take place on the second floor, in an office with wooden flooring. The woman weighed approximately 600 pounds. I greeted her and invited her to sit in a chair like one you might find in a dining room.

The moment she sat down, and I began to pray in preparation for the session, the chair suddenly began to rock violently, moving her back and forth across the room from one corner to the other, as though under the force of an unseen hand. Neither she nor I could stop it. When the chair with her on it reached the far side of the room, I recognized the need to take spiritual authority over the situation immediately. I verbally bound the evil spirits, which were clearly attempting to intimidate or distract us from the task at hand.

Once that was done, we were able to proceed and complete the session successfully. Later, several people who had been on the first floor beneath the room where the deliverance took place told me that the sounds above them were like a horse race thundering overhead.

Case No. 2:

In another instance, I was ministering deliverance to a woman in her mid-sixties. She was bound by a spirit of victimization and a spirit of sickness. It appeared she had grown accustomed to these spirits, perhaps even welcomed them, because they brought her the sympathy and attention of her children and others around her. She constantly complained of illness in one form or another.

As I began casting out the spirits, she suddenly wrapped both hands tightly around her neck and began to squeeze as if trying to suffocate herself. I immediately commanded the spirit to release her. It responded with chilling defiance: "I will kill her before I let her go."

At that moment, the Holy Spirit revealed to me that the woman needed to renounce the spirit of victimization. Once she did so, the demon would have no more hold on her, because it did not own her. I led her through a prayer of renunciation, and as soon as she renounced those oppressive spirits, they released their grip. She was free.

I also reminded the spirit, again, that it had no ownership over her. Therefore, it had no authority to take her life.

Although demons are deceptive, manipulative, and fiercely resistant, they never win. They are always cast out—provided, of course, that the Holy Spirit leads the minister and is spiritually prepared for the task at hand.

Isaiah 57:15

Satan attacks the spirit because God dwells with a man of a right spirit. He also sends revival through and to a man of right spirit: For thus saith the high and lofty One that inhabiteth eternity, whose name is Holy; I dwell in the high and holy place, with him also that is of a contrite and humble spirit, to revive the spirit of the humble, and to revive the heart of the contrite ones.

What is the Definition of Deliverance?

The general definition of *deliverance* refers to the act of spiritual warfare conducted on a territorial level to cast out demons or evil spirits from an individual. It involves breaking and canceling curses, whether generational, territorial, or self-imposed. This spiritual freedom is made possible because Jesus granted us the authority and power to do so when He brought the Kingdom of Heaven to earth, visibly demonstrated through His casting out of demons, and died on the cross to forgive the sins of all humanity. Deliverance liberates believers from demonic oppression and influences of every kind. Deliverance ministers and ministries focus on dismantling spiritual strongholds in a person's life. Deliverance fosters inner healing from past trauma, abuse, or pain, ultimately guiding them toward a victorious life in Christ.

Believer's Preparation for Deliverance

Before scheduling a deliverance session, it is recommended that the believer prepare themselves both spiritually and physically. The deliverance minister should advise the individual to fast for a day or two, as led by the Holy Spirit. It must also be confirmed that the person is not pregnant, is genuinely willing to be set free from sin, and is prepared to abandon sinful habits. Repentance, the act of forgiving those who have caused harm, and renunciation of all known sins are critical steps. The believer should also be willing to fully cooperate with the Holy Spirit and the minister and arrive promptly for the appointment.

On the day of the session, the minister must first ensure that the individual seeking deliverance has accepted Jesus Christ as their Lord and Savior, or is willing to do so at that time. They must be led to renounce all known sins, as well as any covenants with the world, with sin, the devil, or the flesh. This includes turning away from sexual sin or any other habitual sin, repenting wholeheartedly, and renouncing it with guidance from the minister. The person must confess, without reservation, that Jesus is the Lord of their life and be ready to surrender every idol or area of disobedience— anything or anyone elevated above Christ.

A believer who has genuinely received Jesus as Lord has also received the promise and fullness of the Holy Spirit. Therefore, they should be filled with faith, ready to repent, and willing to renounce all forms of sin, sexual or otherwise, as they prepare to receive deliverance.

If it becomes evident that the individual has not fully embraced or understood the redemptive work of Jesus Christ—salvation, deliverance, inner healing, and physical healing—this is the moment to minister to them in a way that helps them grasp the meaning of Christ's work. Invite them to accept and confess Jesus as Lord. Encourage faith, not fear; trust, not doubt. Emphasize that this journey is grounded in God's love and mercy, not in shame or condemnation. Assure them that any personal disclosures will be held in strict confidentiality. However, unless they make a firm and sincere profession of faith in Jesus as Lord and Savior, the deliverance should be postponed and rescheduled.

John 1:9

That was the true light, which lights every man that cometh into the world.

The second step in deliverance preparation is guiding the believer to forgive every person who has ever harmed them, regardless of how deep the wound or how much time has passed. Deliverance addresses emotional wounds and trauma from every stage of life: infancy, childhood, adolescence, and adulthood. Forgiveness is central to this process.

Scripture makes this clear:

Mark 11:25

Whenever you stand praying, if you have anything against anyone, forgive him so that your Father who is in heaven will also forgive your transgressions and wrongdoings.

Matthew 6:14-15

If you forgive others their trespasses, your heavenly Father will also forgive you. But if you do not forgive others, then your Father will not forgive your trespasses.

Forgiveness is such a foundational requirement that without it, the process of deliverance cannot move forward. An unforgiving heart grants demons legal ground to remain and retaliate, which could hinder or even reverse the intended breakthrough.

At this point, it is essential to teach the believer that forgiveness is not an emotion but a decision—an intentional act of obedience to God. The Bible presents forgiveness as a divine command, not merely a suggestion. Pray with the individual, asking the Holy Spirit to reveal anyone they have not yet forgiven or toward whom they harbor negative, critical, or resentful thoughts.

Encourage them to make a list of such individuals. Then, one by one, walk through the process of forgiveness by naming the offense and the pain caused. Lead them in verbal forgiveness until they can genuinely bless each person. Only then proceed to the next name on the list.

Besides gathering the believer's general information and background, the deliverance minister will also ask discerning and targeted questions related to the following areas:

1. Generational Curses – These may include territorial, bloodline, or personal curses that could be affecting the believer's life and spiritual well-being.

2. Issues of Rejection – From early childhood to the present, covering the three major aspects: the root of rejection, self-rejection, and fear of rejection.

3. Self-Esteem Challenges – Exploring feelings of insecurity, inadequacy, or worthlessness and identifying where and how these began.

4. Mental or Emotional Struggles – Whether personal or inherited through family bloodlines.

5. Involvement with Witchcraft and the Occult – These practices create spiritual barriers and separate individuals from God.

6. Moral and Sexual Integrity – Topics to be addressed include impure thoughts or behaviors such as pornography, fornication, adultery, homosexuality, lesbianism, bestiality, exhibitionism, prostitution, abortion, incest, sexual fantasies, masturbation, rape, and child abuse, among other defiling practices.

The believer should be lovingly encouraged to respond truthfully, with a repentant heart and a sincere desire to walk through the process of deliverance. This honesty is crucial for breaking chains, nullifying curses, and revoking every legal right previously granted to the enemy—whether knowingly or unknowingly by the believer or their ancestors.

Any sin left unconfessed—whether due to forgetfulness, omission by the minister, or reluctance on the part of the believer—will remain an open door for demonic influence. This is highly inadvisable, as it allows the enemy to maintain a foothold in the believer's spirit and soul.

Therefore, it is strongly recommended that the minister utilize a Deliverance Questionnaire to ensure thoroughness and accuracy in this spiritual examination.

Preparation of the Deliverance Minister

Luke 4:18

"The Spirit of the Lord is upon me, because he hath anointed me to preach the gospel to the poor; he hath sent me to heal the brokenhearted, to preach deliverance to the captives, and recovering of sight to the blind, to set at liberty them that are bruised."

Everyone called by Jesus is given the authority to cast out evil spirits. However, certain spiritual qualifications are essential for the minister to operate effectively in this calling. A deliverance minister must live in submission to God and to the earthly authorities He has established—namely, their pastor or apostle. This posture of obedience ensures that demons submit and depart when commanded to leave.

Additionally, the minister must maintain an intimate, ongoing relationship with the Lord, be filled with the Holy Spirit (as evidenced by speaking in tongues), and lead a disciplined life of fasting and prayer. True submission must be to God alone, as submitting to any worldly or ungodly influence can open doors for the devil.

Deliverance sessions should be led by one experienced and spiritually mature minister, accompanied by one or two intercessors who are praying in tongues. These intercessors should be focused on calling for the Holy Spirit's guidance and discerning the spiritual dynamics of the session. They must not interfere unless specifically invited to do so by the lead minister. There can be only one leader, as demons will not respond obediently to divided authority.

Begin every session by inviting the presence of the Holy Spirit through prayer. The opening prayer should also include spiritual precautions—binding spirits of violence, retaliation, accusation, or any other harmful manifestation. From the outset, the minister should summon angels and command them to stand guard, protecting everyone involved in the session.

Keep in mind that during manifestations, a demonized individual may display supernatural strength, rendering physical control difficult. Yet, our authority in Christ is far more powerful than human strength. It is by this spiritual authority that demonic manifestations are subdued.

Psalm 91:11–12 (KJV) assures us:

"For he shall give his angels charge over thee, to keep thee in all thy ways. They shall bear thee up in their hands, lest thou dash thy foot against a stone."

This promise affirms that God dispatches His angels to guard and protect those who trust in Him from harm or danger.

Hebrews 1:14 further explains:

"Are they not all ministering spirits, sent forth to minister for them who shall be heirs of salvation?"

Angels are divine servants, sent to support and assist believers, especially in spiritual warfare.

Finally, the minister should break the power of the afflicting spirits, command the oppression to loosen, and ensure it happens without harming the believer. They should break the demonic alliances and networks, cutting off their lines of reinforcement and severing the connections that give them strength and coordination.

Discernment (word of knowledge) is essential to determine whether the issue at hand stems from the flesh, demonic influence, or a combination of both. The latter is often the case when the problem has persisted over a long period. However, one must never assume this; instead, there must be a clear, prayerful leading and guidance from the Holy Spirit. This should be accompanied by the pleading of the blood of Jesus, the power of the Word, the God-given authority of the ministers, and faith. These tools remain powerful throughout the deliverance session—especially the name of Jesus, the name above every name.

The central focus of the deliverance must be directed toward binding, loosing, and casting out the strongman. The demons subordinate to him must also be bound, loosed, and cast out—or commanded to leave with him—and directed to an appropriate destination. Most often, they are sent to stand at the Cross of Calvary to await judgment. A firm command should be issued, instructing them never to return to the individual who has been delivered.

Competence in ministering deliverance is developed through time, experience, and consistent practice.

Nevertheless, one must always seek the guidance and prompting of the Holy Spirit, who teaches us all things and directs our paths. For training, it is advisable to begin by assisting someone who possesses a degree of experience from whom you can learn and be mentored. Deliverance should never be undertaken without an intercessor committed to praying throughout the entire session. Some sessions may take up to three hours to complete. If, however, demonic manifestations or physical blockages hinder the progress, it may be necessary to pause and resume the deliverance within a week or sooner, though such cases are rare. In most circumstances, the process is completed within a single three-hour session.

Throughout the session, continuous prayer and the seeking of the Holy Spirit's direction are imperative. The Holy Spirit should be asked frequently for revelation, discernment, and insight into what He desires to accomplish as the session unfolds. Ministers should pay close attention to the person's face and eyes, instructing the individual to maintain eye contact. The eyes, often referred to as the windows to the soul, can reveal much about a person's internal condition. Demonic manifestations—such as facial contortions—are commonly observed, especially with spirits of lust, anger, rage, fear, anxiety, and similar influences. Conversely, once a person has been fully delivered, the peace that has been achieved by the person being ministered to should also manifest. Looking at the person's face and eyes is more effective than asking them how they feel because sometimes it's the demons responding, not the person. Demons are deceiving and will provide answers that contradict what one sees in their appearance and demeanor. Statements like "I feel better" or "I have a slight headache or pain here or there" typically indicate that complete freedom has not yet been achieved and that demons may still be hiding in areas of physical discomfort. Full deliverance is evident when the person expresses a deep sense of relief and freedom, often describing the sensation as if a heavy weight has been lifted or as though they are walking on clouds. Their faces radiate with joy, and they express heartfelt gratitude to both the Lord and the ministers. God's work is always complete—never partial. Therefore, the person will truly feel whole.

It is crucial to remind the individual that deliverance is an expression of God's love and mercy—it is not earned by merit but received through confident faith in Christ. This distinction must be understood clearly. Do not conclude the session until there is clear confirmation from the Holy Spirit that the individual is truly free from the influence of the spirit. When attuned to the Spirit, this confirmation can be deeply sensed. At that point, pray over the believer, especially to fill the house—their inner being—so it is not left clean yet empty. An unfilled space invites the return of spirits, often with even greater torment. Instead, pray for the fullness of the Holy Spirit, ask for the gifts of the Spirit to be imparted, declare the joy of the Lord as their strength, and proceed as the Spirit leads.

Deliverance sessions can become exhausting and prolonged if ministers rely on their strength, knowledge, or effort, or if they allow the individual being ministered to stray off-topic when answering questions. Encourage direct and concise responses to maintain spiritual focus. This is why the presence of a trained and knowledgeable leader is essential, while those being trained should primarily observe and intercede in the Spirit.

Above all, remain in the Spirit, fully aware that apart from Jesus in our hearts and the empowering presence of the Holy Spirit, we can accomplish nothing.

Once the session concludes, close in prayer by thanking the Holy Spirit for His presence and guidance. Give Him all the glory and honor. Then, bind all spirits of vengeance and retaliation against everyone present. Bind potential attacks such as accidents, illnesses, job loss, or any form of harm. Claim divine protection over each individual's family, finances, health, and employment. Once more, remain sensitive and obedient to the leading of the Spirit of the Lord.

Finally, give clear instructions on how to maintain their deliverance. It is essential to follow up with the believer periodically, encouraging them to remain connected to the body of Christ, attend church regularly, and be accountable to at least one trustworthy person, preferably a spiritual mentor. Explain the warning found in Matthew 12:43-45:

Matthew 12:43-45

"When an unclean spirit goes out of a man, he goes through dry places, seeking rest, and finds none. Then he says, 'I will return to my house from which I came.' And when he comes, he finds it empty, swept, and put in order. Then he goes and takes with him seven other spirits more wicked than himself, and they enter and dwell there, and the last state of that man is worse than the first. So shall it also be with this wicked generation."

Ministering Self-Deliverance

The believer should not be permitted or encouraged to practice self-deliverance unless he is fully convinced of his salvation and completely committed to his faith. Moreover, he should have undergone at least one prior deliverance session with a minister. He must affirm that Jesus Christ is his Lord and Savior and that, by faith, he has renounced all sinfulness, demonic covenants, worldly attachments, and curses. His commitment to follow Jesus for the rest of his life should be resolute. He must also demonstrate full control over his faith, emotions, actions, and behavior.

Self-deliverance is most appropriate for mature Christians who, having fallen into sin in a specific area, have sincerely repented and now desire to pursue a life marked by holiness, service, and consecration unto the Lord. Individuals who are emotionally overwhelmed or under psychological distress should refrain from attempting self-deliverance.

The New Testament Greek word for salvation, *sozo*, means healing. Every act of deliverance contributes to inner healing—this is significant because the Lord often uses the circumstances of deliverance to cultivate faith, deepen love, and foster trust and confidence in Him, all for His glory.

That said, the believer's mentor or pastor must ensure that the individual's actions align with biblical principles, are time-tested, and are effective in achieving lasting freedom. Any practice that ventures into extra-biblical revelation should be avoided. The believer must be especially vigilant, as Satan is eager to lure him into unbiblical, emotionally driven, or ineffective methods—ultimately resulting in counterfeit deliverance experiences. Such theatrics serve to delay genuine freedom and rob God of His glory. As Apostle Paul warns us in Scripture, we must not be ignorant of the enemy's devices. Satan loves a spectacle. Do not allow it. When demonic manifestations are permitted to become theatrical, it distracts from the Lord's work and glory.

Surrender every part of your life to the Holy Spirit—including your thoughts and bodily members. Begin by confessing your sins to the Lord, repenting, and renouncing the iniquities that prompted your need for deliverance. Recommit to holiness, then pray:

Heavenly Father, my life, my thoughts, my heart, and all my body belong to You. I commit my emotions and all my hidden parts to You and humbly ask You to enter every innermost part of me and remove every demon I have renounced. I command every demon hiding within me to expose itself and come out of my body now, in the name of Jesus.

Take a deep breath, collect yourself, and be attentive to any physical sensations, such as pain, tingling, or numbness, that may indicate demonic activity. Conclude the session with a prayer to the Holy Spirit, asking Him to fill you with His presence, surround you with His protection, and cover you with His glory. Let Him guide you as He wills.

An unbeliever must never attempt self-deliverance.

Each person seeking deliverance should walk through the following steps:

RECEIVE – Receive healing and deliverance by accepting Jesus Christ as Lord and Savior through grace. It cannot be earned; you cannot labor to obtain it. It is a gift.

REVIEW – Examine your current spiritual state. See, there are no blocks to deliverance, such as unwillingness to give up the sin and repent.

REPENT – The believer who falls into sin needs to repent conscientiously to be free. It is the open door to the rest of the inner healing and deliverance process.

RENOUNCE – Renouncing will pave the way for restoration and prosperity.

REMIT – The problem must be remitted to the Lord, as Grace is needed. Attempts to control behavior through self-effort often perpetuate the issue.

RELEASE – Release all sense of anger, resentment, bitterness, unforgiveness, hate, or other sinful feelings such as self-loathing or any other feelings.

REQUEST –If you remain in me and my words remain in you, ask whatever you wish, and it will be given to you.

REFUGE –Faith Confession: "Jesus saves those who take refuge at His right hand, from their enemies.

REBUKE – The Holy Spirit warns us to take every thought into captivity and to cast down every vain imagination.

RESIST – Scripture commands us to resist Satan and, having done all, to stand.

REMIND – The person seeking deliverance from sin must stay close to the Lord by walking in the Spirit. This will keep him/her from doing the things of the flesh.

1 Peter 5:8–9

"Be self-controlled and alert. Your enemy, the devil, prowls around like a roaring lion looking for someone to devour. Resist him, standing firm in the faith..."

James 4:7

"Submit yourselves, then, to God. Resist the devil, and he will flee from you."

Why Some People Do Not Receive Deliverance

It is possible for someone to undergo deliverance and still not experience freedom. This may result from various causes, with perhaps the most significant being a reluctance to surrender fully to God's truth. If the individual has not genuinely proclaimed Jesus as Lord or if they lack understanding of the deliverance process, the session will not be fruitful.

Some people attend deliverance reluctantly, saying, "I came because my spouse made me." Such individuals lack a true desire to be set free, and this disinterest blocks the process. Continuing in sinful relationships or environments that foster darkness will further hinder deliverance. Unconfessed sins give demons a legal right to remain. Moreover, unforgiveness, lack of faith, and unbroken demonic alliances all serve as obstacles to complete freedom.

Prayer Of Salvation

Romans 10:9–13

That if you confess with your mouth the Lord Jesus and believe in your heart that God has raised Him from the dead, you will be saved. For with the heart, one believes unto righteousness, and with the mouth, confession is made unto salvation. For the Scripture says, "Whoever believes in Him will not be put to shame." For there is no distinction between Jew and Greek, for the same Lord is rich to all who call upon Him. For "whoever calls on the name of the LORD shall be saved."

PRAYER

Heavenly Father, I recognize that I am a sinner and that my sins separate me from You. Today, I voluntarily repent of my sins and ask for Your forgiveness. I confess with my mouth that Jesus is the Son of God and that God the Father raised Him from the dead. Jesus, I ask You to enter my heart, enter my life, and cleanse me with Your blood. I accept You as my Lord and Savior. I break every covenant I made with the world, the devil, and my sinful past and make a new covenant with You, Jesus, for all eternity. When I die, I know I will be in Your presence in heaven. Thank you, Jesus—I am saved, and I am free. In Jesus' name, AMEN!

Chapter 6
Soul Care and Inner Healing

1 Thessalonians 5:23

"May the God of peace Himself sanctify you completely, and may your whole spirit, soul, and body be preserved blameless at the coming of our Lord Jesus Christ."

God's purpose in creating humans in His image and likeness was to have them reflect His nature in every aspect of their lives on earth. His divine intent was to replicate Himself in a created being who carried His 'spiritual DNA,' maintained intimate communion with Him, ruled over His creation, and fulfilled His command to be fruitful, multiply, and fill the earth.

(Supernatural Deliverance, Maldonado, p. 46)

However, none of these divine assignments can be carried out effectively until man is restored to God's original design. As we now understand, sin has marred humanity's reflection of God's image and likeness. Yet, through the process of deliverance, inner healing, and the ongoing transformation by the Holy Spirit within, restoration is not only possible—it is promised. One can stand on that promise because, *"God is not a man, that he should lie; neither the son of man, that he should repent: hath he said, and shall he not do it? Or hath he spoken, and shall he not make it good?"* Numbers 23:19

Exodus 15:26-27

"And said, If thou wilt diligently hearken to the voice of the LORD thy God, and wilt do that which is right in his sight, and wilt give ear to his commandments, and keep all his statutes, I will put none of these diseases upon thee, which I have brought upon the Egyptians: for I am the LORD that healeth thee."

Every person on earth was created with a purpose, and within that purpose, God has already placed all that is needed: resources, finances, skill sets, wisdom, knowledge, and the right destiny helpers. But this purpose must first be discovered—and that discovery lies within the heart of the Creator and the discovery of the unique talents He has bestowed upon each individual to fulfill that purpose.

By now, you may have already torn down the sinful or evil altars exposed in your life, as outlined in Chapter 2. Perhaps you have presented a new altar—one of commitment, righteousness, and worship—before the Throne of Grace. After engaging with Chapter 3, you may have broken generational, territorial, and bloodline curses. You may have already experienced deliverance, as discussed in Chapters 4 and 5.

The next step is inner healing. Total healing is not accomplished in a single session of ministry, deliverance, or counseling. Inner healing and soul care address the sinful responses and false beliefs that take root in our hearts during painful life experiences. These are often deeply buried reactions, formed during childhood and usually linked to our families of origin, especially our parents.

These ingrained reactions are frequently negative and abrupt, often marked by anger. They arise because we lack the tools or emotional maturity to respond appropriately to traumatic or inappropriate events during the early stages of our lives. When deeply hurt, we may struggle to articulate our pain and confusion. As a result, we formed ungodly judgments, blamed ourselves or others, and developed responses rooted in rejection or fear of abandonment.

Because these emotional patterns begin early, they can persist through adolescence and into adulthood—unless we receive deliverance and inner healing. Carrying this pain within a broken heart disrupts not only our earthly relationships but also our relationship with ourselves and, most critically, with our Heavenly Father. It prevents us from fully loving and respecting ourselves, others, and God as we were created to.

The truth is, everyone needs inner healing. Every person has experienced pain—often inflicted by parents, caregivers, siblings, teachers, or peers. Unless these wounds are processed in a timely and healthy way—and most of us have not done so—we carry them for years, even decades. But when you encounter the healing power of Jesus Christ and begin to explore the blessings of soul care, something changes. You find relief. You discover peace. You experience joy. You undergo a complete transformation of the soul.

Until that transformation begins, however, many develop a poor self-image. You might blame yourself for imagined flaws or exaggerated imperfections. In trying to soothe your internal pain, you may turn to addictions or destructive habits that offer momentary comfort. Many of these tendencies have already been addressed in previous chapters.

The following three behaviors or reactions are signs that something in our hearts needs attention and that all is not well within our souls:

We feel angry whenever we think about people or events from our past.

We experience strong overreactions to situations that are relatively minor or insignificant.

We encounter repeated patterns of negative experiences in life, resembling a curse.

These angry feelings, exaggerated responses, and recurring patterns represent the negative consequences that manifest in our lives. This bad fruit is rooted deeply and must be removed at its core—permanently. Why? Because you were created by your Heavenly Father, who designed you with purpose: to live a life filled with promise, blessings, peace, joy, and fruitfulness. His desire is for you to prosper in every area of your life.

Psalm 1:3–4

He shall be like a tree planted by the rivers of water, that brings forth its fruit in its season, whose leaf also shall not wither; And whatever he does shall prosper. The ungodly are not so, but are like the chaff which the wind drives away.

If emotional injuries are not addressed promptly and thoroughly, they result in a broken heart. This brokenness manifests through symptoms such as intense sadness, anxiety, isolation, low self-esteem, fear, rejection, distrust, anger, and more. These wounds become embedded in your memory—even if you think you've forgotten them. Eventually, your reactions betray the presence of these buried hurts, emerging unexpectedly and damaging your relationships and well-being.

In Chapter 5, we explored the Deliverance process, during which you are set free from generational curses, a broken heart, rejection, physical and psychological issues, unforgiveness, witchcraft and the occult, and moral struggles—including sexual sin. All of this can occur in a three-hour session or longer. During deliverance, every form of demonic oppression and influence is expelled from your life, and their return is only possible if the door is reopened through sin, unforgiveness, or re-inviting the curse.

Inner healing, by contrast, addresses emotional and spiritual wounds through faith-based practices and techniques. These may include Christian counseling, meditating on Scripture, surrendering burdens to the Lord, and allowing Him to perform the deep work of restoration. Soul Care offers a holistic path to emotional and spiritual wellness, centered on intentional living and alignment with your values and God-given purpose. These are not one-time events; they are processes that unfold over time and must be embraced as ongoing journeys.

Matters of the heart must be addressed *in the Spirit*, through the discernment and guidance of the Holy Spirit.

True heart-healing takes time; it is a transformative journey that produces a renewed and restored you. As the emotional residue of pain, fear, anxiety, anger, and unforgiveness begins to fade, something beautiful takes root. In their place, new emotions, attitudes, and perspectives emerge—those born of the Spirit. You begin to surrender more deeply to the Holy Spirit and to bear His fruit: love, joy, peace, long-suffering, kindness, goodness, faithfulness, gentleness, and self-control.

This surrender marks the resurrection of a new self, while the old self—the part of you you're not proud of and perhaps struggle to love—gradually fades away. Why does this transformation happen? Because when you gave your life to Jesus Christ and made Him the Lord of your life, you were filled with His Spirit. The Holy Spirit took up residence within you. That very day, you became a new creation in Christ Jesus. You were saved, and your name was written in the Book of Life. A divine shift occurred in Heaven. Your destiny changed. You were blind in the darkness, but now you see—the light of Jesus shines on your path.

If you were to die today, your spirit would enter Heaven without question. But while you are still here on Earth, you are called to undergo this transformational process. Not only does it heal every hidden wound, but it also leads to the renewing of your mind—a process that changes the way you think, behave, and respond to life. After all, your thoughts shape your attitudes, and your attitudes shape your behavior.

As you may have heard, your attitude determines your altitude. And if you've ever dreamed of soaring, this is your moment. Because with Jesus, nothing is impossible.

Romans 12:1–2

I beseech you, therefore, brethren, by the mercies of God, that you present your bodies a living sacrifice, holy, acceptable to God, which is your reasonable service. And do not be conformed to this world, but be transformed by the renewing of your mind, that you may prove what is the good and acceptable and perfect will of God.

2 Corinthians 5:17 (NASB)

Apostle Paul says that, "If anyone is in Christ, he is a new creature; the old things have passed away; behold, new things have come."

Apostle Guillermo Maldonado, in his book Supernatural Transformation of the Heart, teaches that "although our heart is the center of our being, many people do not truly understand the heart and how it functions" (Supernatural Transformation, p. 9). He does not refer to the physical organ but to the "inner man," or spirit. Scripture further tells us in Jeremiah 17:9 that "The heart is deceitful above all things, and desperately wicked; who can know it?" Yet, the transformation I speak of here takes root in the surrendered and changed heart.

Every believer is in the ongoing process of becoming more like Jesus—a process known as sanctification. Above all other callings, our highest aim is to reflect Jesus in our lives. This pursuit spans a lifetime, for none of us consistently lives up to our best selves, let alone fully emulate Christ. There may be fleeting moments where Jesus is reflected in our actions, only to be followed by periods where we fall short. And so, we press forward—one day at a time—always grateful that His mercies endure forever.

In the book of Ephesians, Paul exhorts the church:

"Get rid of all bitterness, rage and anger, brawling and slander, along with every form of malice. Be kind and compassionate to one another, forgiving each other, just as in Christ God forgave you" (Ephesians 4:31-32, NIV).

How can Christians be instructed to "get rid of" these things unless they still exist, even after salvation? Because the reality is that we all remain in need of spiritual refinement. We are given opportunity after opportunity to grow and be perfected as we commune with the Holy Spirit.

Embracing spirituality means experiencing God in every dimension of our being and recognizing the interconnectedness of body, soul, and mind. Tending to your emotional and spiritual well-being is an act of worship—it honors God. True transformation is the full restoration of God's image in us. It is holistic salvation—not only does God forgive sins and heal the visible consequences, He also restores what has been damaged in the depths of our inner man. This includes traumas caused by our actions, thoughts, and behaviors, as well as those inflicted upon us by others, even from childhood.

Inner healing and soul care are ultimately about surrender—giving God full access to work within us. Without the Holy Spirit's active presence, it is nearly impossible to break spiritual chains, shatter yokes, or heal deep emotional wounds. Only the Spirit can replace the heart of stone with a heart of flesh, one filled with love and compassion.

The only plea to the reader of this book is this: be humble enough to sit at the feet of the Master. Allow Him to be your Deliverer, your Healer, and the tender Shepherd of your soul—even in the areas where your understanding has fallen short. He knows the condition of your soul even better than you do. He will guide you—whether to seek counseling, receive guidance from a pastor, or remain still and allow Him to work with you personally.

Yet know this: He will not do the work alone. God invites your partnership. He desires your surrender, your time, and your intentional faith. He calls you to voluntarily release worldly habits, walk away from ungodly relationships, abandon religious posturing and traditions, and loosen your grip on materialism, which serves to weigh you down and hinder your spiritual progress.

Psalm 46:10

Be still, and know that I am God; I will be exalted among the nations, I will be exalted in the earth!

Prayer

Heavenly Father, as I finish this book, my prayer is that it will glorify *You*, the Most High and precious Lord of all ages. I pray it *brings glory to Your* name as it reaches the hands of men and women who are *desperately seeking* a transformational breakthrough in their lives. *May they* receive it, and *in turn, be inspired* to follow *Your path toward* deliverance, healing, and restoration of *everything* the enemy *has stolen from* them.

I pray that their spirits and souls have a profound encounter with Your presence and the fullness of the Holy Spirit—that they would never turn back. I declare that their eyes will be fixed on what lies ahead, focused on Your glorious Kingdom of righteousness and justice.

In Jesus' name I pray. Amen.